An Anthology of Ancient Mesopotamian Texts

An Anthology of Ancient Mesopotamian Texts

When the Gods Were Human

Sabine Franke

PEN & SWORD
ARCHAEOLOGY

First published in Great Britain in 2016 by
Pen & Sword Archaeology
an imprint of
Pen & Sword Books Ltd
47 Church Street
Barnsley
South Yorkshire
S70 2AS

© Original Edition *Als die Götter Mensch waren. Eine Anthologie altorientalischer Literatur* (2013) by Philipp von Zabern, an imprint of WBG (Wissenschaftliche Buchgesellschaft), Darmstadt, Germany

ISBN 978 1 47383 434 7

Typeset in Ehrhardt by
Mac Style Ltd, Bridlington, East Yorkshire
Printed and bound in the UK by CPI Group (UK) Ltd,
Croydon, CRO 4YY

Pen & Sword Books Ltd incorporates the imprints of Pen & Sword Archaeology, Atlas, Aviation, Battleground, Discovery, Family History, History, Maritime, Military, Naval, Politics, Railways, Select, Transport, True Crime, and Fiction, Frontline Books, Leo Cooper, Praetorian Press, Seaforth Publishing and Wharncliffe.

For a complete list of Pen & Sword titles please contact
PEN & SWORD BOOKS LIMITED
47 Church Street, Barnsley, South Yorkshire, S70 2AS, England
E-mail: enquiries@pen-and-sword.co.uk
Website: www.pen-and-sword.co.uk

Contents

Preface

'When the gods were human' – the beginning of the Old Babylonian tale of the deluge refers to a mythical period of time before mankind, when the gods had to do all chores themselves. They created humanity to ease their burden. How the people in the ancient Near East – modern Iraq and Syria – viewed and went about their lives is shown in the extraordinarily diverse and extensive literature of the region, which has been written down since about 2000 BC and preserved throughout the centuries in temples, palaces and private residences.

Ancient Near Eastern literature beyond the famous Gilgamesh epic is still awaiting discovery by a wider readership. From a wealth of material, predominantly narrative texts have been chosen for this anthology.

After the gods created mankind in the tale of the deluge, the god Enlil was so irritated by their noise that he threatened to eradicate them in a flood. However, the most wise Atramhasis survives the great flood due to the help of the god of wisdom, Ea. Parallels with Biblical motifs are unmistakable here, as they are in the tale of the incredible rise of King Sargon, the child abandoned on the river who became a ruler. The tale of the deluge later became part of the Gilgamesh epic, in contrast to the conflict between the ruler Gilgamesh of Uruk and King Akka of Kish presented here.

An invocation of the tooth worm against toothache, against the crying of a baby; a plea for relief from debts, and a dialogue about the indifference of the gods (the Babylonian theodicy) show the day-to-day engagement of ordinary people with the world and the gods. A dialogue between a master and his servant, who always agrees with him, contains – all satire aside – a discussion of the question of what constitutes a meaningful life.

In fairytales such as the story of the revenge of a pauper on an arrogant mayor, or the search of King Etana for the herb of fertility, which carries him on the wings of an eagle up into the sky, desires, fears and dreams are moulded into a timeless literary form.

The goddess Ishtar is the mightiest goddess of the ancient Near Eastern pantheon. She is able to journey into the underworld to attempt to defeat this 'land without return'. King Ammiditana of Babylon addresses himself to this awe-inspiring goddess in one of the most beautiful hymns of the ancient Near Eastern literature, as he asks her to grant the authority for his rule. Ishtar/Inana is also the focus of a unique text in which the high priestess Enheduana desperately tries to avoid her fate. In another text King Utuhengal of Uruk reports, with pride and rich imagery, his success against the invading Gutian hordes.

The translations are based on the academic editions listed in the respective notes, but they use their own free, interpreting phrases and amendments to facilitate understanding. Only few texts of Akkadian and Sumerian literature are preserved completely. Gaps in the texts are marked, regardless of their extent, by '…', and amended and uncertain passages are in italics. Text (in round brackets) has been added for better understanding.

I am greatly indebted to the translators, who collaborated promptly and willingly, and who despite many other obligations have produced easily readable and intelligible translations, each with footnotes and a bibliography.

Students have a rough ride at times – we can probably all recognise the problems, vexations and disappointments of a student. One student's labours and sufferings provide the final tale in this volume – a small compensation for the efforts of all the scribes to whom we owe these texts.

Sabina Franke

When the Gods were Human: The Ancient Near Eastern Tale of the Deluge

Rosel Pientka-Hinz

(The world order of the gods: early years)

When the gods were human they carried the hardship, they hefted the hamper.

The hamper of the gods was large, the hardship great, excessive were the tribulations.

The great Anunnaku let the Igigu bear the hardship sevenfold.

Anu, their father, was king; their advisor was the hero Enlil. Their throne-bearer was Ninurta, their inspector of the canals Ennugi. They clasped the bottle (for casting lots) by its 'cheek', cast the lot whereupon the gods apportioned [the spheres of influence]:

Anu ascended to the sky, *Enlil took* the earth for his *subjects*.

The bolts and the meshes of the sea were placed before the far-seeing Enki.

Those of Anum ascended to the sky, *those* of the (groundwater) Apsu descended forever.

Idle were those of the sky, *they let* the Igigu bear *the hardship*.

8

The gods began to dig *rivers – the streams of the gods*, life for the land.

The Igigu began to dig *rivers – the streams of the gods*, life for the land.

The gods dug the river Tigris and then *the Euphrates.*

They opened springs in the depths of the groundwater, *wells ...* they founded.

... (the groundwater) Apsu, ... of the land.

... amidst it, they elevated its tips.

They heaped up the mountains, *the years* of the conscription to labour *they counted.*

They set up the great swamp, *the years* of the conscription to labour they counted.

(The rebellion of the Igigu)

For *2,500* years in excess *the gods* bore the hardship day and night.

(Then) they sat down and began to berate (each other); [they] muttered in the pits:

'Come, we will apply to the throne-bearer so that he takes away our great hardship from us!

The god, the advisor of the gods, the hero – come, we will lift (him) from his seat!

Enlil, the advisor of the gods, the hero, come, we will lift (him) from his seat!'

We opened his mouth and spoke to the gods, his brothers:

'*Let us beat* the throne-bearer of old times; ... *will appoint Enlil!* ... *another he will appoint, ... before us....*'

9

(We incite the gods further)

'The advisor of the gods, the hero – come, we will lift (him) from his seat!

Enlil, the advisor of the gods, the hero – come, we will lift (him) from his seat!

Now call out for the fight, we will stage a battle!'

The gods listened at his behest, they put fire to their tools,

They set fire to their shovels, put their hampers to the torch.

They clasped each other when they approached the gate of the sanctuary of the hero Enlil.

It was night at half-watch, the house was surrounded, the god does not know [it].

It was night at half-watch, the Ekur was surrounded, Enlil does not know [it].

Yet then Kalkal took note (and) let all be locked, he seized the bolt, checked the gate.

Then Kalkal awakened *Nusku*, they heard the clamour of the *Igigu*.

And Nusku awakened *his master*, let him rise from the sleeping berth:

'My lord, surrounded is your house, the fight is fast approaching *your gate*.

Enlil, surrounded is your house, the fight is fast approaching your gate.'

(Thereupon) Enlil let *weapons* be brought into his apartment.

Enlil opened his mouth and spoke to the vizier Nusku: 'Nusku, bolt your gate, take your weapons (and) step before me!'

Nusku bolted his gate, took his weapons, stepped before Enlil.

Nusku opened his mouth and spoke to the hero Enlil: 'My lord, (pale as) a tamarisk is your face; these are (nevertheless) your own children, why have you become (so) alarmed?

Send (someone) to bring down Anu and (also) Enki shall be fetched for you!'

He sent (someone), Anu was brought down, and Enki was fetched for him.

There he sat, Anu, the celestial king; the king of the (groundwater) Apsu, Enki, *remained in one position.*

The great Anunnaku were present, Enlil rose and the case was *presented.*

Enlil opened his mouth and spoke to the great gods:

'Have they really risen against me? Do I have to commence battle *with my own children?* You gods, what do I have to witness? The fight rushed towards my gate!'

Anu opened his mouth and spoke to the hero Enlil:

'The cause for the Igigu having surrounded (you) at your gate – *Nusku* may go forth and *find it out!*

The instruction *he shall announce* to your sons…!'

Enlil opened his mouth and spoke to the *vizier Nusku*:

'Nusku, open *your gate*, take your weapons *and go outside to the group!*

In the assembly *of all (those) gods* kneel down, (then) announce yourself *(and) repeat our instruction*:

'I was sent by *your father Anu*, your advisor, *the hero Enlil,* your throne bearer *Ninurta* and your *inspector of the canals Ennugi (with the words):*

11

'Who *is the god responsible for this fight?* Who *is the god responsible for the onslaught?* Who *has instigated* the riot? (*So that) the fight could approach the gate* of Enlil.'

Nusku opened his *gate, took his weapons and went outside with* Enlil's *instructions. In the assembly of* all (those) gods *he knelt down, (then) announced himself and* conveyed *the commandment:*

'*I was sent by* your father Anu, *your advisor,* the hero Enlil, *your throne bearer* Ninurta, *and your inspector of the canals* Ennugi (with the words):

'Who *is the god responsible for this fight?* Who *is the god responsible for the onslaught?* Who *has instigated the riot?* (So that) the fight *could approach* Enlil's *gate.'*

In *the assembly the Igigu answered,* they were incensed … :

'Each of *us gods declared this war;* we staged *our gathering* in the *pits.* The oversized hampers (*nearly) killed us,* great was *our hardship and excessive our tribulations!*

And so the mouth of each *of us gods* created *the fight with Enlil* collectively.'

Nusku took *the reply,* went away *and spoke to his master:*

'My lord, where you have sent me – I went *to the* numerous gods, delivered *your* great *instruction.* The entirety *of the Igigu rose up:*

'Each of us gods declared the war! We staged our *gathering* in the pits. The oversized *hampers* (nearly) killed us, *great was* our hardship and excessive the tribulations!

And so the mouth of each of us gods created the fight with Enlil collectively.'"

When Enlil heard this word, his tears were flowing.

Enlil *internalised* his speech, he spoke to the hero Anu:

'My prince, *carry away with* you *the divine order* up *to the sky, take your* power ...!

With the Anunnaku seated before you call forth the one god and the divine order shall be renewed!'

(The creation of mankind)

Ea opened his mouth and spoke to the gods, *his* brothers:

'Of what do we accuse them? Great was their hardship, excessive the tribulations.

Day by day the earth was ...; the clamour was loud *and we could hear the calling!*

There is *work to do*, there sits Belet-ili, the womb.

The womb may create the *primordial man* and (henceforth) man shall heft the hamper of god!'

The goddess they called, they asked the midwife of the gods, the wise Mami:

'You are the womb, the creator of mankind, make up the primordial man, (henceforth) he shall bear the yoke! The yoke he shall bear, the work of Enlil; (henceforth) the hamper of god shall be hefted by man!'

Nintu opened her mouth and spoke to the great gods:

'With me (alone) it must not be done, but together with Enki it is a deed!

He (in particular) purifies anything; the loam he may give to me and (then) I (also) wish to do it!'

13

Enki opened his mouth and spoke to the great gods:

'On the first, seventh and the fifteenth day of the month I will carry out the purification, (namely) a bathing!

The one god shall be slaughtered and the gods shall purify themselves right in the middle of it!

With his flesh and his blood Nintu shall mix the loam!

God and man shall be blended together with the loam!

For all future days we will hear the drum (heart) beat sound; (for) in the flesh of the god the We spirit may reside!

The living he shall let his sign to be known, *(for) in order to not* let *(it)* be forgotten, the We spirit may be present!'

In the assembly the great Anunnaku answered with 'yes', the guardians of the fates.

On the first, seventh and fifteenth day of the month he carried out the purification, (namely) a bathing.

We, the god who had understanding, they slaughtered in their assembly.

With his flesh and and his blood Nintu mixed the loam.

For all future days *he will let the drum (heart) beat be heard*, (for) in the flesh of the god *was* the spirit. The living he let his sign to be known, (for) in order to not let (it) be forgotten, the spirit was present.

When she (Nintu) had mixed the loam, he (Enki) called the Anuna, the great gods.

The Igigu, the great gods, spit saliva onto the loam.

Mami opened her mouth and spoke to the great gods:

14

'The task you had assigned me to do and I have completed it.

The god you have slaughtered together with his mind.

Your great hardship I have removed, our hamper [I have] settled onto man!

(Thus) you have bestowed lament onto mankind;

(For you, however,) I have loosened the neck ring (and thus) caused (your) liberation!'

They heard this her speech (and) ran around free, kissed *her feet*:

'Previously *we called you* 'Mami'; now Belet-kala-ili 'mistress *of all gods*' shall be your name!'

Then *the house of fate* was entered by the far-seeing *Enki (and) the wise* Mami.

(The process of human procreation)

…

(It follows the creation of seven male and seven female foetuses. The first man and the first woman grow up, she bears a child.)

… her breasts.

A beard *appears … on* the cheek of the young man.

In the gardens and (on) the streets the wife and her husband courted each other.

The wombs were gathered; (also) Nintu sat there where she counted the months.

In the house of the fates they announced the tenth month.

15

The tenth month came and she put on the *ladies' garment*, opened the womb.

Radiant and joyful was her face, she covered her head, carried out the midwife's duty.

Her (the mother's) hips she girded while she spoke words of blessing.

She drew (a circle) with flour and put down a brick.

'I, I have created, my hands performed (it)! The midwife may rejoice in the house of those dedicated *qadištum*!

Where (ever) a pregnant woman gives birth and the mother of the baby delivers [it], the brick shall be put down nine days long! Worshipped shall be Nintu, [and] the womb (Belet–ili)!

'Mami' she shall (then) call her *sister; she shall praise* the womb, shall put down the (prayer) mat (for her)!

In their houses, when the beds have been made, *the wife* and her husband *may court each other*!

During the time of being wife and being husband Ishtar shall rejoice in the *wedding* house!

Nine days long joy shall prevail, Ishtar shall (then) be called 'Ishhara' (the goddess of love)!

On *the fifteenth day*, at the moment of fate *you shall* name ... *me!*'

...

(Mankind, continuing to multiply, works for the upkeep of the gods)

A man *said* ...: 'Purify the apartment ...!'

The son to *his* father …, ….

They sat down and …; he, he carries ….

He saw and …, Enlil ….

They took …; new hoes and spades they created.

Great dykes they built for (sating) the hunger of mankind, for the food *of the gods.*

(Mankind procreates. Enlil is irritated by their noise and sends a plague to decimate them)

The womb was opened (and) created a baby *(incessantly).*

(The three plagues: first plague)

Not three times 1,200 years *had passed (and) the (inhabited) land became more and more widespread*, the humans more and more numerous.

The land was loud *as (roaring) bulls*, through *(their clamour)* the god became restless.

Enlil had to listen to their racket, *(and) he spoke* to the great gods:

'*Troublesome has become to me* the racket of mankind, *due to* their rowdiness I lack sleep.

Order (it) and an influenza may arise!'

(Enki advises Atramhasis how mankind can be saved from the plague)

Yet (there was) he, *Atramhasis* ('Exceeding in wisdom'); his god was Enki, *his* ear *opened* (attentively).

He speaks with *his* god, and he, his god, *speaks* with *him*.

Atramhasis *opened his* mouth *and* spoke to *his lord:*

'Until *when* ..., do they (actually) burden us with the illness for *ever?*'

Enki opened his mouth *and* spoke to *his* servant:

'Call the elders (for council) in time, (for) *I give you* the (following) advice within the house:

'Order it!' the heralds shall announce, the (/this) call they may proclaim loudly within the land:

'Do not worship your gods, do not pray to your goddess!

(Yet) (the messenger of death) Namtara – his gate you shall visit (and) bring cake and pastries to its front!

An offering of roasted flour may reach him so that he may be shamed by the gifts (and) wipe clean his (disease-causing) hand!'

Atramhasis received the instruction (and) gathered the elders at his door.

Atramhasis opened his mouth *and* spoke to the elders:

'*I called* the elders (for council) in time, (for) *my lord* (Enki) *gave me within* the house the (following) advice:

'*Order it!*' shall the heralds call out, *the/this call* they may proclaim loudly throughout the land:

'*Do not worship* your gods, *do not pray to* your *goddess*!

(Yet) (the messenger of death) *Namtara* – his gate *you shall visit (and) bring cake and pastries to* its front!

An offering of roasted flour may reach him so that he may be shamed through the gifts (and) wipe clean his (disease-causing) hand!'"

The elders heard *his* speech (and) *for* Namtara – in the city they built *his* house.

They ordered (it) and *the heralds* called it out, the (this) call they proclaimed loudly *throughout the land*.

No (longer) they worshipped *their* gods, did *not* pray to *their goddess*.

(Yet) (the messenger of death) Namtara – *his* gate they visited (and) *brought* cake and pastries to *its* front.

The offering of roasted flour reached him, *he was shamed* by the gifts (and) wiped clean his (disease-causing) hand.

The influenza left them (and) *their good faces* returned.

Their previous racket arose (anew).

(Second plague)

Not had passed *three times 1,200* years, (and) the (inhabited) land became more and more widespread, humanity more and more numerous.

The land was noisy as (roaring) bulls, through their clamour the god became restless.

Enlil had to listen to their racket (and) he spoke to the great gods:

'Troublesome has become the racket of the humans to me, due to their rowdiness I lack sleep.

Cut off the food from the humans, for (the sating of) their hunger the plants shall be too sparse!

His rain (the weather god) Adad shall wipe away, to no beneficial effect the abundance of water shall come forth from the depth!

The wind shall blow (and) lay bare the ground!

The clouds may swell up, (yet) the burst of rain [may] not drip down!

The field shall decrease its yield, Nisaba (the grain goddess) shall lock her breasts firmly!

For them (humanity) there shall exist no joy, … shall go up in smoke!'

(Enki's instruction to Atramhasis how mankind can be spared from the drought)

Atramhasis opened his mouth and spoke to the elders:

'*I called the elders (for council)* in time, *(for) my lord (Enki) gave me the (following)* advice *within the house:*

'*Order it!*' shall the heralds *declare*, the/this call *they may proclaim loudly* throughout the land:

'Do not worship your gods, do not pray to your goddess! Yet (the weather god) Adad – his *gate* you shall visit (and) bring cake and pastries *to its front*!

He may receive *the roast flour offering* so that he is shamed *by* the gifts (and) wipe clean his (fatal) hand!

In the morning hours he may let fog precipitate, [he may] steal in already during the night and let rain down the dew!

The field may bear ninefold (furtively) like thieves!'

(The eldest heard his speech and) for Adad – in the city they built his house.

They ordered (it) and the heralds proclaimed it, the (this) call they announced loudly throughout the land.

No (longer) did they worship their gods, did *not* pray to their goddess.

(Yet) (the weather god) Adad – his gate they visited (and) *brought* cake and pastries to its front.

He received the offering of roasted flour, he was shamed by the gifts (and) wiped clean his (fatal) hand.

In the morning hours he let fog precipitate, he stole in already during the night and let the dew rain down!

The field bore (furtively) *like* thieves ninefold.

The drought left them *(and)* their *good faces* returned.

(Third plague)

...

(Enlil sends as a third plague a famine. Atramhasis seeks to commune with Enki in his dreams.)

... gate of his god, ... he sat his foot.

Day by day, again and again he cried, took incense there in the morning hours.

To the wise of the gods he is sworn and *the attention* he directs to the dreams.

To Enki he is sworn and *the attention* he directs to the dreams.

... *in the* house of his god, ... he sat down (and) cried.

... *into the water* he threw, ... he sat down (and) cried.

When the river lay entirely still, he made libations during *the night*.

(When) sleep came *like a twin*, he spoke *to the* river:

21

'The river shall receive *and* carry [it] away, my gift shall be placed before *Enki*, my lord!

May Enki see (it) and think of me! (And) I, *I may have a dream* in the night!'

After *he has sent (it) off on the river, he sat down crying* opposite the river.

On the bank ..., *his favours descended* to (the groundwater) Apsu.

Enki heard *his call, he spoke* to the Lahmu creatures.

'The man who ..., this one may ...!

Go and *bring him* my instruction, ask *him and tell me the matters of his land!'*

...

Above...,

below the abundance of water did not well up from the depth.

The womb of the earth did not bear [fruit], no plant grew (and) humans were not visible.

The (sated) dark floods faded, the steppe land in between was filled with salt.

In the first year they ate the old (grain), in the second year they scraped out the granary.

The third year came and because of hunger their countenance became dark.

Like crusted malt their faces were scabbed, piece by piece their lives came to an end.

Those (once) tall became short of stature, with a low stoop they roamed the street.

The broad-shouldered became slim, their tall stance crumbled.

Messengers took on the assignment (and) traversed (the land) before the seas.

There they stood and started to report to him, the far-seeing Enki, on *Atramhasis'* commission:

'..., ... now you have abandoned me! ... be your wish!'

...

(A renewed salvation of mankind follows, this time possibly initiated through a flood of marine fish. Soon after Enlil announces his wish to destroy the continuously racketing people by a deluge, against which Enki raises objections and provokes a conflict with the other gods.)

(The deluge: assembly of the gods and decision-making)

Full of anger was *he (Enlil) about Enki*:

'The great Anuna, *all of us* – our mouth did bear *the oath* unanimously!

Above Anu monitored (the weather god) Adad (and) I, I monitored the world below.

Wherever Enki went, he loosened the neck ring (and) caused the liberation.

(Thus) he ceded the yield to the humans, placed (*balancing*) ... in the swirls of the sun.'

Enlil opened his mouth and spoke to the vizier Nusku:

'*Two* ... may be led to me (and) let enter before me!'

23

Two ... they led to him, and the hero Enlil spoke to them:

'The great Anuna, all of us – our mouth did bear the oath unanimously!

Above Anu monitored (the weather god) Adad (and) I, I monitored the world below.

Wherever you went, *you loosened the neck ring (and)* caused the liberation.

(Thus) you ceded the yield to the humans, *placed (balancing)* ... in the swirls of the sun.'

...

'(The weather god) Adad *let stream down* his showers of rain, *so that* ... filled the fields and meadows, *clouds* covered ... .

You *shall not* (no longer) feed his people, *nor* provide (the grain of the grain goddess) Nisaba (for) the fertility of men!'

Thereupon *the god* was fed up with (only) sitting there, (and) a (pained) smile niggled at him in the assembly of the gods.

Enki was fed up with (only) sitting there, *(and)* a (pained) smile niggled at him *in* the assembly of the gods.

... evil speech at his hand,

...

... Enki and Enlil.

'*The great Anuna, all of us* – our mouth *bore the oath* unanimously!

Above Anu monitored (the weather god) Adad (and) I, I monitored the world below.

Wherever you went, you loosened the neck ring (and) caused the liberation.

(Thus) you ceded the yield to the humans, *placed (balancing)* … in the swirls of the sun.'

(Nintu:) 'Your hamper *was imposed on man*, (thus) you have bestowed lament *on mankind*.

The god you have slaughtered together with *his mind*, then you sat down and … .

… brought …, *and* your heart *uttered the instruction*:

'They (mankind) shall 'disappear completely'!

We want to bind the leader by oath, the far-seeing Enki!"

Enki opened his mouth *and* spoke to the gods, *his brothers*:

'Why do you wish to bind me by oath …, shall I (actually) raise my hand against *my (own) people*?

The deluge of which you speak *to me* – who [what] is it?

I, I do not know this!

Shall I actually create *the deluge*? The execution of this lies with *Enlil*!

He shall choose each time *and* …, (the twin gods) Šullat and Khaniš may go ahead!

Errakal *shall uproot* the mooring posts, *Ninurta* shall go (and) flood *the land*!'

…

'Assemble …, do not cease …!'

The gods ordered the (final) destruction, the evil deed against mankind was effected by Enlil.

(The building of the ark)

Atramhasis opened his mouth and spoke to his lord:

…

(Atramhasis had a dream about Enki and wishes to learn its meaning.)

Atramhasis opened his mouth and *spoke* to his lord:

'Explain the contents *of the dream* to me, I wish to know its *beginning*, to search for its ending incessantly!'

Enki opened his mouth and spoke to his servant:

'I wish to search incessantly on the sleeping berth!', you say; the message which I will communicate to you heed well!

'Wall, listen to me; reed fence, listen to all my words! Dismantle your house (and) build a boat! Abandon your estate and save your life!

The boat which you will build, … be symmetric!

…

Cover it with large awnings, roof it like the (groundwater) Apsu!

Its interior shall not see the sun, top and bottom shall be covered!

The furnishings shall be reinforced, the bitumen shall be thick, (thus) make it resistant!

(And) I, I will then let it rain for you – an abundance of birds, baskets full of fish.'

He opened the water clock (and) filled it; the course of the flood storm – its seven nights it should announce him.

Atramhasis received the instruction (and) assembled the elders at his door.

Atramhasis opened his mouth and spoke to the elders:

'With your god my god *does not agree*, Enki and *Enlil* rage against each other (and) I was expelled from the city.

(Yet) because I always have worshipped *Enki, he put* these words (*into my mouth*):

'I can *no longer* dwell in *your city*, nor place *my foot on* Enlil's earth.

With the god I will *descend to (the groundwater) Apsu (and) live (there)*!' This he said to me (*my god Enki*).'

...

(The construction of the ark has commenced)

The elders ....

The carpenter *carries his axe*, the reed mat weaver *carries his stone*.

The bitumen *is fetched by a wealthy man*, a pauper *brought what else was needed*.

...

He brings ....

All what he had *in* ..., *(with this) he loaded it up;* all what he had *in* ..., *(with this) he loaded it up*.

Pure (animals) he slaughtered, (namely) *cattle*; fat (animals) *he butchered*, (namely) sheep.

He selected *and let* enter winged *birds* of the sky.

Cattle ..., wildlife ... of the steppe ... he let enter.

... he brought at the (first of the) month, *to* ... he invited his people.

… to the feast … he let enter his family.

While they ate and drank, he went inside and out (again).

He could not sit still and not kneel, broken was his heart and he vomited bile.

(The disaster)

(Then) the face of the day changed, the (weather god) Adad roared inside the clouds.

When they heard the god's clamour, the bitumen was fetched, (and) he began to close his gate.

After he had closed his gate, Adad (still) roared inside the clouds.

The winds raged during his departure, he cut the rope (and) cast off the boat.

…

… the mats.

… the storm, … were tied fast.

(Storm bird) Anzu – with his claws *he tore up* the sky.

… the land, *like clay pots* he smashed its cry.

… *came forth* the deluge; *like* a battle the disaster swept across mankind.

One brother could *not* see the other, they were *not* detectable in the catastrophe.

The deluge was loud like (roaring) bulls, *like* a screaming eagle the storm howled.

Dense was the darkness, there was no sun; *the descendants (died)* like flies.

... *the raging* of the deluge, ... they took.

..., ... the roaring of the deluge.

... *(even) the* heart of the gods *was made* to beat [faster].

Finally Anu lost his temper and his children were dragged before him.

Nintu, the mighty mistress, her lips are totally dried up.

The Anuna, the great gods, sat there with thirst and hunger.

When she saw this, the goddess started to cry, the midwife of the gods, the wise Mami:

'The day shall become gloomy, anew it shall be come entirely dark! In the assembly of the gods – how could I just order with them the (final) destruction?

Had Enlil pressed forward (and) let *my* mouth speak?

Like this (goddess) Tiruru he (possibly) let my mouth rebel?

Well into my (most inner) self and in my body I hear within myself their screams!

Beyond my (*power of imagination*) the descendants (died) like flies.

And I, how will it be to live (perhaps) in a house of lament, (in which) my (own) voice is silenced?

Shall I (perhaps) ascend to the sky (or rather) stay in a house (with nothing but) endangered people?

Where has Anu gone, the master of instructions whose speech the gods, his children, had heard? He who rashly has caused *the deluge* (and) has brought together mankind for the disaster!'

...

Nintu laments …:

'What kind of father would have created this *giant wave?* They (the humans) filled the sea like dragonflies (fill) the river!

Like a raft they washed up at the meadow, like a raft they (also) washed up at the [river] banks in the steppe.

I saw (it) and cried about them, (until) I had exhausted my lamentation of them.'

She cried (anew) and let her heart draw breath.

Without pause Nintu wailed, loudly her feelings expressed themselves. The gods cried with her because of the land.

They became fed up with the lamentation, they thirsted for beer.

(And) where she had settled down to cry, (those also) sat down and like (a flock of) sheep they crowded around the gullet.

Thirsty were their completely dehydrated lips, they trembled incessantly in the pangs of hunger.

Seven days, seven nights the downpour lasted, the storm, *the deluge*.

Where …, … was shed.

(Retreat of the flood and landing of the ark)

To the *four winds* … he put *down an offering*.

It rains …, … .

The gods *smelled* the aroma, *like* flies they were gathered above the offering.

After they had consumed the offering, Nintu rose and complained to all of them:

'Where has Anu gone, the master of instructions?

Did Enlil crowd to the incense offering, he who had rashly caused the deluge (and) gathered mankind for the disaster?

(After all) your mouth brought the (final) destruction, (so that) their (humanity's) light faces became dark (forever)!'

Thereafter she approached (the adornment made of) large flies which Anu had manufactured in presence of the (divine) 'ancestors' [?]:

'Mine (shall be) their lament, it is my fate!

He (Anu) may let me go forth from my misfortune (and) open my face (soothingly)! I will come forth in the *morning* …; in the *land* … .

These flies shall be lapis lazuli (beads) at my throat!

(By this means) I will (forever) commemorate the (these) days…!'

Then the hero *Enlil* spied the boat, he was full of anger against the Igigu:

'The great Anuna, all of us – our mouth did bear the oath unanimously!

From where (then) did (this) creature escape? How could a human survive the disaster?'

Anu opened his mouth and spoke to the hero Enlil:

'Who, if not Enki, could do such thing? A fence of reeds he lets announce the instruction!'

(Thereupon) *Enki* opened his mouth *and spoke* to the great gods:

'*Indeed* I did this in your interest, *I let preserve* the life …!

31

... the *gods* ..., ... the *deluge* ....

... he *caused* ....

Enlil, (...) *let* your heart *draw breath*, ... and relax!

Upon the guilty impose your punishment, *also* upon everyone who wishes to push aside your word!

... the assembly ...

...

... it, ... they put down.

Then I let my heart draw breath!'

(The new world order)

Enlil opened his mouth and spoke to the far-seeing Enki:

'*Now then*, call the womb Nintu, so that you, you and her, can confer in the assembly!'

Enki opened his mouth and *spoke* to Nintu the womb:

'*You (are) the* womb who bears the fates, *(also) create death* for mankind!

There shall be a third among the humans for whom shall ... *be!*

There shall be a third among the humans for whom ...!

Moreover there shall be a third among the humans, among the (these) people a fertile woman (will become) an infertile one!

There shall be among the humans the (she-demon) 'extinguisher', she shall seize the baby from the lap of her who has borne (it)!

Appoint *ugbabtu* priestesses, *entu* priestesses as well as *egisitu* priestesses; they shall be 'untouchable'! (So) restrict procreation!

… those dedicated to *naditum, those dedicated to šugitum* as well as those dedicated to *qadištum*.

…

(Besides further regulations of mankind the conclusion of peace among the gods is addressed.)

'(…) as we have caused the deluge, but one man survived *the disaster*!

You (Enlil) are the advisor of the *great* gods, on *your* instructions I have called forth the fight.

For *your* praise this song may hear the Igigu (and) preserve your great deeds!

About the deluge I sing for all humanity: listen!'

The Tooth Worm

Sabina Franke

After Anu had created *the sky*, the sky had created *the earth*, the earth had created the rivers, the rivers had created the canals, the canals had created the quagmire, the quagmire had created the worm, the worm went crying to Shamash, even before Ea his tears were flowing: 'What have you given me for food, what have you given me to suck upon?' – 'I gave you the ripe fig, the apricot, the apple!' – 'Me? Why, however, the ripe fig, the apricot, the apple? Lift me up and place me between tooth and gums! I wish to suck the blood of the tooth and nibble away pieces of the gums.' – 'Place the hook and seize the root (of the tooth)! Because you say this, worm, Ea shall beat you with his strong hand.'

Invocation against toothache

The treatment (for this): Blended beer, a chunk of malt and oil you shall mix, recite the incantation three times over it (and) place (the mixture) onto the tooth.

Letter of Request to a God

Sabina Franke

To the god, my father, speak: the following is said by Apil–Adad, your servant: Why have you neglected me so? Who could give you someone like me? To Marduk who loves you write so that he ... my debts! I want to see you! I want to kiss your feet! Look upon my family, old and young! For their sake have mercy upon me! Your help shall reach me!

Lullaby

Sabina Franke

Baby who lives in the house of darkness: you have come forth, you have seen *the light of the sun*. Why do you cry, why do you scream? Why did you not cry there?

You have disturbed the household god, the Kusarikkum has awakened: 'Who has awakened me, who has startled me?' – 'The baby has awakened you, the baby has startled you.' Like those intoxicated by wine, like visitors to the tavern it shall be overcome by sleep.

Incantation to calm a baby.

The Master and his Servant

Karin Stella Schmidt

'Servant, approve what I say!' – 'Yes, master, yes!' – '*Go fetch me the chariot and hitch it up* so that I can drive to the palace!' – '*Drive, master, drive!* Set off, they will fail because of you, *the ruler* will be lenient with you.'

'*No, servant, I* won't drive to the palace after all.' – 'Then do not drive, master, do not drive. *The ruler* will send you *into battle*, he lets you take a *route* which you do not know, day and night he will keep doom on hand for you.'

'Servant, *approve what* I say!' – 'Yes, master, yes.' – Fetch water for my hands immediately, I wish to eat!' – '*Eat*, master, eat! Regular meals relax the soul. *Who sates himself with food* is his own god. Shamash accompanies washed hands.'

'No, servant, I won't eat after all.' – 'So do not eat, master, do not eat. To be left hungry and to eat, to be left thirsty and to drink visits man everywhere.'

'Servant, approve what I say!' – 'Yes, master, yes.' – 'Go fetch me the chariot and make it ready so that I can drive to the countryside!' – 'Drive, master, drive! The stomach of a man always roaming is full, a roving dog bites through bones. A *raven* flying around is able to nest, a roaming donkey has enough to eat.'

'Servant, no, I won't drive to the countryside after all.' – 'Then do not drive, master, let it be. The rambler changes his view(s), the *legs* of a roving dog are broken. The home of a raven flying around is a niche in a wall, and the roaming donkey has the pasture as its resting place.'

'Servant, approve what I say!' – 'Yes, master, yes.' – 'I wish to build *a* house *and* have *a son*.' – 'Then do so. A house is *wealth*. … an open door is his/its name. … attentive … is two thirds of a fool.'

'*No*, … I wish to burn, then to stay and to return afterwards, I wish to see it in front of my detractor.' – 'How now?! Look at it, master, look at it.' – 'What – how?! I wish to build a house!' – 'Do not build a house! Go! Now he has destroyed (the good reputation of) his parental home!'

'Servant, approve what I say!' – 'Yes, master, yes.' – 'Now I wish to do something wrong!' – 'What?! Do so, master, do so. If you do not commit robbery, how will you dress yourself? Who will enable you to fill your stomach?'

'No, servant, of course I will not commit a robbery.' – 'A man doing wrong is either dead or tortured or blinded or confined or thrown into prison.'

'Servant, approve what I say!' – 'Yes, master, yes.' – 'I will love a woman.' – 'Love, master, love. A man who loves a woman avoids depression and misery.'

'No, I will never love a woman.' – 'Then simply do not, master, do not love. A woman is a well – a cistern, a hole, a ditch. A woman is a sharp iron dagger cutting the throat of the man.'

'Servant, approve what I say!' – 'Yes, master, yes.' – 'Quickly, fetch water for my hands so that I can prepare an offering for my god.' –'Offer, master, offer. The man who prepares an offering for his god is content inside: he gains more and more benevolence.'

'No, servant, I will not offer to my god!' – 'Then do not offer, master, do not offer. Otherwise you teach your god that he will run after you like a pet dog – and he will repeatedly demand something from you, either ritual acts or cult figures or other things.'

'Servant, approve what I say!' – 'Yes, master, yes.' – 'I will work as a lender.' – 'So lend, master, give (grain) loans. Who gives credits as lender, his grain remains his own and nevertheless he has very high interest.'

'No, servant, I certainly won't give loans as a creditor.' – 'So let it be, master, do not give loans. To give loans is like the love (for) a woman, to get them back (the loans) is like having children. They eat your grain, let the interest on your grain disappear and then, then they continuously abuse you.'

'Servant, approve what I say!' – 'Yes, master, yes.' – 'I will nurture my land.' – 'Nurture it, master, nurture it. Who nurtures his land (publicly) his good deeds are noted by Marduk.'

'No, servant, by no means will I support my land.' – 'Then desist, master, do not nurture it. Go up to the old hills and walk about there, there look at the skulls of the ones who sooner or later have deceased: who of them was an evildoer, who a benefactor?'

'Servant, approve what I say!' – 'Yes, master, yes!' – 'So what is good?' – 'To break my neck and thine, and to be thrown into the river, that is good! Who is so tall that he might ascend to the sky? Who is so wide that he might embrace the earth?'

'No, servant, I will kill you and let you go to your death before me.' – 'Then my master will certainly not survive me three days.'

The Revenge of the Poor Man of Nippur

Sabina Franke

There once was a man from Nippur who was weak and poor. Gimil-Ninurta was his name; he was a very sorrowful man. In his city of Nippur he lived in toil, for he had no silver, as was common for people like him. He had no gold, a characteristic of mankind. His storage jars lacked pure grain, with the desire for food he pined away, with the desire for meat and beer his visage was very distressed. Every day he lay about hungry, without food, only with a single garment without substitution he was dressed.

Woefully he held council with himself: 'I could take off my garment without substitution and (with it) buy a sheep in the marketplace of my city Nippur.' He took off his garment without substitution and bought a three-year-old goat in the market of his city Nippur. Unhappily he held council with himself: 'I could slaughter the goat on my premises, but there would be no feast, for where would be the beer? (Furthermore) my neighbours would hear it and be furious. My family and clan would be angry with me. I will take the goat and bring it to the mayor's house. Something good and nice I will achieve for my stomach with this.'

Gimil-Ninurta seized his goat by the neck and *went* to the gate of the mayor of Nippur. To Tukulti-Enlil who guarded the door he said: 'Announce that I wish to enter and see the mayor!' The gate keeper said to his master the words: 'My lord, a citizen of Nippur waits at your gate and as a gift … he brought you a goat.' The mayor was furious with Tukulti-Enlil: 'Why *is* a citizen of Nippur *standing* at the gate?' The gate keeper … to … .

Gimil-Ninurta came merrily before the mayor. When Gimil-Ninurta stepped before the mayor, he held in his left hand the neck of his goat, with his right hand he greeted the mayor: 'Enlil and Nippur shall be a blessing for the mayor! Ninurta and Nusku shall let his descendants thrive!' The mayor spoke to the citizen of Nippur the words: 'What wrong has happened to you that you are bringing me a gift?' Thereupon Gimil-Ninurta told his wish to the mayor: 'Every day I lie about hungry, without food. I took off my garment without substitution and *at the place* of my city Nippur I bought a three-year-old goat. *Unhappily* I said to myself: 'Suppose that I slaughter the goat on my premises, then there would nevertheless be no feast, for where would be the beer? (Furthermore) my neighbours would hear it and they would be furious. My family and my clan would be angry with me. *To the house of the mayor* I wish to bring my goat.' That was what *I have pondered.* …' (The mayor probably orders the goat to be slaughtered, to be served and then says:)

'Give him, the citizen of Nippur, a bone and a tendon, water him with third-class beer from your canteen, throw him out and chase him from the gate!' Then he gave him, the citizen of Nippur, a bone and a tendon, then he watered him from his canteen with third-class beer, then he threw him out and chased him from the gate.

When Gimil-Ninurta emerged from the gate, he said to the porter who guarded the door the words: 'To your master the greetings of the gods! Tell him the following: because of this one burden you have placed upon me – this one I will pay you back three times!' The mayor heard this and laughed the whole day.

Gimil-Ninurta set off for the palace of the king: 'By the king's order! Prince and governor will (certainly) pass a just sentence!' When Gimil-Ninurta entered the prince's place, he fell down before

41

him and kissed the ground in front of him. He raised his hands and greeted the king of the world: 'Ruler, ornament of mankind, king who makes the guardian spirit famous: a chariot shall be given to me on your order so that I receive for one day all which I desire. For my one day (of use) my payment will be one mina of the finest gold.' The prince did not ask: 'What is actually your desire that you *wish to drive around* in a chariot a whole day long.' They gave him a new chariot fit for a nobleman, they girded him with a new belt, ... He mounted the new chariot fit for a nobleman. Then he set off for *his* city of Nippur.

Gimil-Ninurta caught two birds, stored them in a box and sealed it with a seal. Then he trekked to the gate of the mayor of Nippur. The mayor went out to him: 'Who are you, my lord, you who travels ...?' – 'The king, your lord, has sent me, ... For the Ekur, Enlil's temple, I bring gold.' In order to be able to offer him a sumptuous meal the (mayor) slaughtered a premium sheep. The mayor ... before him: 'Ooh, am I tired and ... . Gimil-Ninurta spent the first watch of the night next to the mayor, until the mayor, who was very exhausted, was sound asleep. Gimil-Ninurta rose in the middle of the night like a thief, opened the hatch of the box, *so that the birds flew up to the sky*. 'Mayor, get up! ... the box! The hatch of the box is open! The gold has vanished!' Gimil-Ninurta ripped his garment, as it was his plan, approached the mayor and let him raise his hands in supplication. From his head to the soles of his feet he pummelled him and caused him pain. The mayor beneath him cried out in fear: 'My lord, you are not allowed to kill a citizen of Nippur. With the blood of a protected citizen which is sacred to Enlil you shall not stain your hands.' They made him a present of two minas of red gold; in place of his garment ripped by himself he gave him another.

When Gimil-Ninurta emerged from the gate, he spoke to Tukulti-Enlil guarding the door the words: 'For your lord the blessings of the gods! Tell him the following: because of the one burden *you have placed*

42

upon me: the first I have paid you back. *Two remain.*' The mayor heard this and *brooded* the whole day.

Gimil-Ninurta visited a barber. He shaved off all his hair … . He filled a soot-blackened skillet *with water*. He set off for the gate of the mayor of Nippur. To the door keeper guarding the gate he said: 'Announce that I wish to enter and see the mayor!' – 'Who are you who wishes to see him?' – '*I am* a doctor from Isin who examines … . The position of illness and wounds … .' When Gimil-Ninurta entered the mayor's house, he showed him the injuries which he (Gimil-Ninurta) himself had inflicted on him. The mayor said to his servants: 'The doctor is capable.' – 'My lord, only in the dark my remedies work, in a secluded, far removed location.' He brought him to an inaccessible place where no friend or companion could have compassion for him. He threw the skillet right into the fire (and doused it). He drove five stakes into the firm ground and tied him at the hands, feet and head. From the head to the soles of his feet he pummelled him and caused him pain.

When Gimil-Ninurta emerged from the gate, he spoke to Tukulti-Enlil guarding the door the words: 'On your lord the blessings of the gods! Tell him the following: because of the one burden which *you have placed upon me*: Two I have paid you back, so that only one remains.'

Gimil-Ninurta was excited. Like a dog *he pricked up his ears*, he watched all men, he looked at all the people. A man *he sent forth – he had received all his expenses* – and gave him *a goat* as his gift: 'Go to the gate of the mayor *of Nippur … and* emit a loud cry. At your cry all men will come together from everywhere, (and you will shout) '*I have returned* to the mayor's gate! I am the one with the goat!' Gimil-Ninurta *crouched under* the bridge like a dog. The mayor emerged at the shouting of the man. He let the servants of his house come out, women and men – they all swarmed out to look for the man. While all were on the search for the man, they left the mayor behind in the open in solitude. Thereupon Gimil-Ninurta jumped out from under the bridge and seized the mayor. He approached the mayor and made him beg for mercy. From his head to the soles of his feet he pummelled him and caused him pain. 'Because of the one burden you have placed upon me: three times I have paid you back for it.' He left him behind and went out into the steppe. The mayor could reach the city only by crawling.

The Tale of Etana

Karin Stella Schmidt

The great gods (planned and) designed a city, the great gods laid *the foundations*, they planned the mighty city of *Kish*, the great gods laid its foundations. The Igigi made (all) its mud brick buildings to last, a king shall be its shepherd … Etana shall be its architect … the shepherd's crook … . The great Annunaki *who decide the fates* … sat and conferred about their decisions *for the lands. They created* the four corners of the world … . On the order of all, the Igigi *designated* the *man* … . A king they had not (yet) appointed over the innumerable people … . At this time *no tiara was yet bound and no crown manufactured*, no sceptre was (yet) decorated with lapis lazuli (blue) (and) in the regions not a single sanctuary was (yet) built. The Sebettu closed *the gates* before man and in front of the villages and towns they closed … . The city was enclosed by the Igigi … . Ishtar *looked for* a shepherd … and for a king she looked everywhere … . Inanna *looked for* a shepherd … and for a king she looked everywhere … . Enlil examined the (cult) plinth of sky *and earth* … . The young man Etana was named by Ishtar. She searched continuously *and intensively*, in the land a king *shall be designated, in Kish* … . The kingship … he brought … the gods of the lands … . His *wife spoke* to him, (to Etana): '… let me *see* a *dream*. As *for* Etana my death is *determined* … as yours, (so) *also is my death determined* … . Etana, the king, *will die after me*. His shade *appeared* before *me* … , but in the palace he is not *visible*.'

…

45

... man his name ... he built a *tower* ... . The base of Adad's throne, his god ..., in the shadow of this sanctuary grew a *Euphrates poplar*. In its crown an eagle resided, *inside its roots a serpent* was curled up. Daily they watched *each other*. The eagle opened his beak and said *to the snake*: 'Come, let us two make friends, oh let us be friends – you and I!' *The snake* opened his mouth *and said to the eagle*: '... he who ... a friendship *before Shamash* ... . If you commit an evil deed, you *hurt* his feelings, [you] break a taboo of the gods *and [you] stir the god's wrath*! Come, we will ready ourselves and climb up the mountains, we will swear on the *wide* earth!' Before the hero Shamash they swore an oath: who *transgresses* Shamash' boundary, Shamash shall *hand over* mercilessly to the thug's hands! Who *transgresses* Shamash' boundary, for him the access routes *to the mountains* shall close themselves off! The looming weapon may *come down* on him, the laws of the oath before Shamash may catch up with him and *take him prisoner* (with snares)!

When they had sworn the oath on the *wide* earth, they readied themselves and climbed up to the mountains. For one day each they watched prey, the eagle caught wild bull or onager, the snake fed (on it), (then) turned away (so that) his young could feed. The snake captured mountain goats and gazelles, the eagle fed (on it), (then) turned away (so that) his young could feed. The eagle seized wild bucks and wisents, the snake fed (on them), (then) turned away (so that) his young could feed. The snake caught animals of the steppe and wildlife of the earth, the eagle fed (on them), (then) turned away (so that) his young could feed. The *eagle's* young *ate* the provender (by which) the eagle's young had become large and had grown (tall).

When the eagle's young had grown up and grown tall, the eagle planned evil in his heart, he planned (truly) evil deeds in his heart: he intended to eat the young of his companion! The eagle opened his beak and said to his young: 'I wish to eat the serpent's young – the snake *dwells amidst the earth*, (yet) I ascend and reside in the sky and

46

only fly down to eat *fruit* in the boughs of the trees!' A small young – exceeding in wisdom – spoke to his father, the eagle, the warning: 'My father, do not eat (them)! Shamash' net will entrap you! The laws of the oath before Shamash will catch up with you and *capture* (you with snares)! Who transgresses Shamash' boundary, Shamash hands over mercilessly to the hands of the thug.' (Yet) he did not listen to it, did not listen to *the warning of his young*. He flew down and ate the serpent's young.

In the evening, in the middle of the day's course, the serpent came, he carried meat as a burden. At the entrance of his *nest he lay down the meat* and discovered that his nest *was empty*! He checked, not .... *the eagle* had *raked* the ground with his talons, above the dust stirred up (by the eagle's flight) *clouded* the sky. The snake *lay* down and wept, before Shamash *its tears were flowing*: 'Hero Shamash, I have trusted you! For the eagle I have provided ... . Now my nest has become a place of lamentation, my nest *is no longer, his nest (in contrast) is safe and sound*! My young have vanished, *his young are alive and well*! He descended and ate *my young*. Shamash, the evil he has done to me, *you know it well*! Shamash, for certain your net is *the wide earth*, your traps are the *ample* sky! The eagle, the evildoer – the Anzu! – who does *evil to his companion*, may by no means escape your dragnet!'

When he *heard* the pleading of the snake, Shamash opened his mouth and said to the serpent: 'Go along the path, roam through the mountains, where I have bound a wild bull for you. Open its intestines, *slit open its belly*, arrange your waiting place *inside its belly*. All the birds of the sky will descend and eat the meat, (also) the eagle will *come* with them ... If he does not know (anything) ..., he will carefully select the soft parts of the meat (for himself), he will approach again and again *with appetite*, will bore through to the abdominal skin. When he reaches the inside, you will seize him by his wings. Clip his wings, his feathers and his pinions! Pluck him, throw him into a pit without *bottom – he shall die* the death of hunger and thirst!'

47

On the instruction of the hero Shamash the serpent went and roamed through the mountains. The snake arrived at the wild bull, he opened its inside, *slit open* its belly, arranged his waiting place in its stomach. All birds descended from the sky and ate meat, (only) the eagle – does he know of his danger? Does he not feed with the young birds on the meat? The eagle opened his beak and spoke to his young: 'Come! Let us fly down and eat the meat of this wild bull!' A small young – exceeding in wisdom – gave to its father, the eagle, the warning: 'My father, do not fly down – perhaps the serpent lurks in the inside of this wild bull!' The eagle considered by himself: '*If* the birds *were terrified* how *can it be that* they are eating the meat *so peacefully*?!' (Therefore) he did not listen to it, did not listen to the warning of his young. He flew down and settled on the wild bull. The eagle examined the meat, checked from the front and from the back. He examined the meat a second time, checked its front and its rear. Again and again he moved around *with appetite* and (then) bored through to the abdominal skin. When he reached the inside, the snake seized him by his wings: '*Into my nest you have broken in, my nest you have invaded*!' The eagle opened his beak and said to the snake: 'Have mercy upon me, like a groom I will give you a (lifelong) dowry!' The snake opened his mouth and said to the eagle: 'If I let you go, (then) how will I satisfy Shamash above? He will (then) turn your punishment against myself, the punishment which I (now) place upon you!' He clipped his wings, his feathers and his pinions, plucked him and threw him into a pit without *bottom* (so that) he should die the death of hunger and thirst.

The eagle *thrown into the pit* turned daily again and again to Shamash: 'If I die in the pit, will everybody know (then) that I was inflicted with your punishment? Let me, the eagle, live! Your name I will proclaim forever!' Shamash opened his mouth and spoke to the eagle: 'With your evil deeds you have hurt my feelings, a taboo of the gods, an unforgivable deed you have committed! You may die, with you

I will not grapple (any longer). (Yet) a man whom I will send to you is coming and he will help you!'

Daily Etana turned again and again to Shamash: 'Shamash, you have eaten the fat of my sheep, the earth has drunk the blood of my lambs! The gods I have honoured, was reverent against the shades! The female dream readers have used up my incense; my lambs have been used entirely by the gods through slaughter. (My) lord, on your word – give me the herb of childbirth! Show me the plant of fertility! Erase my shame, assign me a name/son!' Shamash opened his mouth and spoke to Etana: 'Go along the path, roam through the mountainside, be on the look-out for a pit, look into it! An eagle is thrown into it, he will show you the herb of childbirth.' On the instruction of the hero Shamash Etana went, *roamed through the mountainside*, kept a look-out for the pit, looked into it: *the eagle was thrown* into it ... . Immediately he lifted him up ... .

...

The eagle opened his beak *and said to his lord Shamash the word*: 'My lord, ... *The language* of a bird *is not like that of man.* I am a bird – *he is a man.* Everything he says *I have understood,* everything I say *he has understood.*' According to the statement of the hero Shamash ... . *The speech* of the bird *Etana has understood.*

The eagle opened his beak and said: 'Speak, why have you come here?' Etana opened his mouth and spoke to the eagle: 'My friend, give me the herb of childbirth, show me the plant of fertility! Erase my shame, assign me a name/son!' 'I will leave ... the herb of childbirth. *The bird* ... in its *exit* ... *there where* it comes forth from *the earth. Take* ... for me. All by myself I will *go and search the* mountains, I wish to fetch you the *herb* of childbirth ... !'

He went (off) *into the mountains, he rose up.* The eagle chased about, *then he returned: 'In the mountains the herb of childbirth* does not exist! Come, my friend, *I will take you up into the air!* With the lady Ishtar *the herb will be available*, to the lady Ishtar *I will bring you! Lay* your arms *upon my wings, lay your hands* upon my feathers!' He lay *his arms* upon his wings and lay *his hands* upon his pinions. A 'double hour' *he carried him upwards*: 'My friend, have a look at the land – how does it appear to you?' – 'The people of the land *buzz like flies* and the capacious sea is on the whole (only as large as) a cattle pen!' A second 'double hour' *he carried him upwards*: 'My friend, have a look at the land – how does it appear to you?' – 'The land has turned into a garden patch ... and the capacious sea is on the whole (only) a box!' A third 'double hour' *he carried* him *upwards*: 'My friend, have a look at the land – how does it appear to you?' – 'I look – (yet) the land I cannot see; and also the capacious sea my eyes cannot discern! My friend, do not rise (farther) into the sky! Turn around on the path of flight! I wish to return to my city!' A 'double hour' he threw him down, and (at this) the eagle fell (likewise) and caught him with his wings. A second 'double hour' he threw him down, and (also herein) the eagle fell and caught him (again) with his wings. (At the distance of) three cubits from the ground *he threw him down*, and (even thereby) the eagle fell (too) and caught him with his wings ... the eagle beat ... from Etana ... .

The city of Kish weeps ... in its interior ... I sang ... Kish ... Etana ... Kish ...

...

... in his house, he reached his city and his house. ... opened his *beak* and said to Etana: '... herb of childbirth. ... earth ... its exit I have seen. ... in order to cook (it) ... . Etana ... he did not fear. ... the god's utterance ... he has reached ... he wished to do ... he unties. ... body of water.

...

Etana opened his mouth and said to the eagle: 'My friend, *this god has shown me clearly in a dream*: we went through the gateway (of the gods)

50

Anu, Enlil and Ea, together we, you and I, prostrated ourselves. We went through the gateway (of the gods) Sin, Shamash, Adad and Ishtar, together we, you and I, prostrated ourselves. I saw a house, I opened *its (door) seal*, its wings I threw open, I entered. Inside a single *young woman* was sitting, adorned with a crown and with a beautiful face. A throne was erected there, Ishtar/a female deity …, at the bottom of the throne lions *were resting*. I rose – and the lions attacked me! I woke up and was (still) frightened … .'

The eagle said to him, to Etana: 'My friend, your dream is very clear: come, I will bring you to the sky of Anu! Rest *your breast* on my breast, lay *your hands* on my wings, lay your arms on my pinions!' He rested *his breast* on his breast, he laid his *hands* on his wings and he laid his arms on his pinions. He *held* his increased burden *firm*, a 'double hour' he carried him upwards, (then) the eagle opened his beak and said to Etana: 'My friend, have a look at the land – how does it appear to you?' Look at the sea, have a look at its coasts!' – '(Verily) the land reaches (directly) up to the mountains and the sea has become a puddle!' A second 'double hour' he carried him upwards, (and then) the eagle said to him, to Etana: 'My friend, have a look at the land – how does it appear to you?' – 'The land … the *body of water* … .' A third 'double hour' he carried him upwards, (and then) the eagle said to him, to Etana: 'My friend, have a look at the land – how does it appear to you?' – 'The sea has become the duct of a gardener!'

When they had ascended to the sky of Anu, they went through the gate of Anu, Enlil and Ea, the eagle and Etana bowed down together. They went through the gate of Sin, Shamash, Adad and Ishtar, the eagle and Etana *bowed down together*. He saw a house, opened its (door) seal, its wings he threw open, *he entered*.

…

(The end of the tale is missing so far.)

51

Invitation to the Dead for a Feast: Ishtar's Descent to the World of the Dead and Dumuzi's Return to the World of the Living

Annette Zgoll

On the land without return, the *great* earth – Ishtar, daughter of Sin, she bent her thoughts on it. The daughter of Sin bent her thoughts on this:

on the dark house, the dwelling of (the goddess of the underworld) Irkalla,

on the house which one, once having entered, does not leave again,

on the path from which there is, once one has set foot on it, no return,

on the house in which one, once having entered, does not see light any more,

where dust is nourishment, loam is food.

Light they do not see, in dark *they squat*, [they] carry plumage like birds.

On door and bolt dust is gathering.

When Ishtar reached the gate of the land without return, she began to say a word to the gate keeper:

'Hey porter! Open your gates for me!

Open your gate for me so that I can enter, do you hear:

It is me!

If you do not open the gate for me – and I – I myself – cannot enter,

then I will hammer down the door, break the bolt,

then I will smash the doorpost, will let the doors crash down.

The I will let the dead ascend, they will devour the living,

more numerous than the living the dead will become!'

The gate keeper opened his mouth and started to talk, started to speak to the great, to Ishtar:

'Be patient, my lady, do not destroy it, wait inside (in the gateway) until the door *will be opened*!

I will go and announce your mission to the queen Ereshkigal!'

Now the gate keeper went inside and started to talk to Ereshkigal:

'Alas, that one, your sister Ishtar, she stands inside the *gate*,

she who possesses the great skipping ropes, who stirs up the Apsu before Ea, *her father*!'

When Ereshkigal heard this, her face became so pale – like a cut tamarisk branch –

that her lips stood out darkly like the rim of a *kuninu* vessel (coated with bitumen):

'What (good) has her heart (ever) brought to me, in what matter has her inclination (ever) made me radiantly happy? What does she want! I, I actually drink only water with the Annunaku!

For food I have just loam, my beer is murky water. I want to weep over the young men who leave their wives!

I want to weep over the young women who are torn from the lap of their husbands!

Over the little child I want to weep who was sent away untimely!

Go, gate keeper! Open the gate for her!

Treat her according to the old rituals!'

The gate keeper went, he opened the gate for her:

'Enter, my lady! (The city of the dead) Kutha may rejoice about you!

The palace of the land without return may be glad because of you!'

The first gate he let her enter, then he removed the great *aga* crown from her head and carried it away.

'Why, gate keeper, have you taken the great *aga* crown away from my head?'

'Enter, my lady! Such are the rituals of the mistress–of–the–earth!'

The second gate he let her enter, then he removed the loops from her ears and carried them away.

'Why, gate keeper, have you taken the loops away from my ears?'

'Enter, my lady! Such are the rituals of the mistress–of–the–earth!'

The third gate he let her enter, then he removed the necklace of ovoid stone beads from her neck and carried it away.

54

'Why, gate keeper, have you taken the necklace of ovoid stone beads away from my neck?'

'Enter, my lady! Such are the rituals of the mistress-of-the-earth!'

The fourth gate he let her enter, then he removed the cloak pins from her chest and carried them away.

'Why, gate keeper, have you taken away the cloak pins from my chest?'

'Enter, my lady! Such are the rituals of the mistress-of-the-earth!'

The fifth gate he let her enter, then he removed the belt with the stone of childbirth from her hips and carried it away.

'Why, gate keeper, have you taken away the belt with the stone of childbirth from my hips?'

'Enter, my lady! Such are the rituals of the mistress-of-the-earth!'

The sixth gate he let her enter, then he removed the rings from her hands and feet and carried them away.

'Why, gate keeper, have you taken away the rings from my hands and my feet?'

'Enter, my lady! Such are the rituals of the mistress-of-the-earth!'

The seventh gate he let her enter, then he removed the robe of honour from her body and carried it away.

'Why, gate keeper, have you taken away the robe of honour from my body?'

'Enter, my lady! Such are the rituals of the mistress-of-the-earth!'

As soon as Ishtar had descended to the land without return, Ereshkigal saw her and trembled before her.

Ishtar did not hesitate, above Ereshkigal she placed herself.

Ereshkigal opened her mouth and started to speak, to Namtar, her vizier, she started to say a word:

'Go, Namtar, take her with you so that she is no longer above me!
Let go forth 60 *diseases so that they overpower* Ishtar!
Disease of the eyes against her eyes,
disease of the arms against her arms,
disease of the feet against her feet,
disease of the innards against her innards,
disease of the head against her head
let out against her, against any part of her, against *her body*!

After Ishtar, my lady, *had descended* to the *land without return,*

– the cow is no longer mounted by the bull, the donkey does not mate with the jennet,

the girl on the street is not impregnated by the young man –

thereupon the young man lay inside his house (alone),

the young woman lay all by herself.

Papsukkal, the vizier of the great gods – bowed to the ground was his face, his countenance *was veiled*, he wore a mourning dress, he wore the hair dirty and tangled.

That one now stepped exhausted before Sin, his father, while weeping, while before King Ea his tears were flowing:

'Ishtar has descended into the underworld – she has not ascended again!

Since Ishtar has descended to the land of no return,

– the cow is no longer mounted by the bull, the donkey does not mate with the jennet,

the girl on the street is not impregnated by the young man –

thereupon the young man lay inside his house (alone),

the young woman lay all by herself.'

Ea – from his wise heart he thereupon created a man.

Indeed he created Asushunamir ('Whose appearance is radiant'), the Assinnu:

'Go, Asushunamir, to the gate of the land without return turn yourself!

The seven gates of the land without return may be opened for you!

Ereshkigal may see you and may beam happily because of you.

When her heart calms down, her soul is gladdened, then let her swear unconditionally, that is to say an oath on the great gods (that she will fulfil a wish for you)!

Then raise your head and scout for a water container!'

(In the following it has to be imagined how the Assinnu reaches the underworld and how Ereshkigal offers him a present, after he has made her happy, which Asushunamir rejects.)

(Asushunamir:) 'No, my lady, (I do not want this)! However, this water container, it shall be given to me! The water therein I want to drink ceaselessly!'

When Ereshkigal heard this,

she slapped her thighs, bit into her finger:

'You have desired something of me, which one does not wish for!

Go, Asushunamir, I will curse you with a great curse:

bread out of those (droppings) from ploughing the seed of the city shall be your food!

The water storage for the irrigation of the city shall be your drinking vessel!

The shadow of the wall shall be your residence wherever you are standing!

Thresholds shall be your abode wherever you are sitting!

The drunk and the thirsty – each shall slap you on the cheeks!'

Ereshkigal opened her mouth and started to talk, to Namtar, her vizier, she began to say a word:

'Go, Namtar, knock at the firm palace!

The thresholds adorn with white pregnancy stones.

The Anunnaku let come forth, on thrones of gold let them have a seat!

Sprinkle Ishtar with the water of life and lead her before me!'

Thereupon Namtar went, knocked at the firm palace.

The thresholds he adorned with white pregnancy stones.

The Anunnaku he let come forth, let them have a seat on thrones of gold!

Ishtar he sprinkled with the water of life and led her before Ereshkigal.

(Addition in the text from Assur)

'Verily – now go away, Namtar! Lead Ishtar away at last!

If she does not give you any person as her replacement, then bring her back here!'

58

Thereupon Namtar led her *to the gates.*

The first gate he let her pass, then he returned to her the robe of honour from her body.

The second gate he let her pass, then he returned to her the rings from her hands and from her feet.

The third gate he let her pass, then he returned to her the belt with the stone of childbirth from her hips.

The fourth gate he let her pass, then he returned to her the cloak pins from her chest.

The fifth gate he let her pass, then he returned to her the necklace of ovoid stone beads from her neck.

The sixth gate he let her pass, then he returned to her the loops from her ears.

The seventh gate he let her pass, then he returned to her the great *aga* crown from her head.

(Anunnaku:) 'If she does not give you any person as her replacement, then return her to her (= Ereshkigal)!

Concerning Dumuzi, the husband of her youth:

With pure water wash him, with good oil anoint him!

In a red-golden garment dress him, a flute of lapis lazuli he shall play!

Whores may distract his thoughts!'

(The description of how all this is made to happen is left out. Also the death of Dumuzi can only be extrapolated indirectly, through the reaction of his sister Belili.)

His sister Belili had put on all her jewellery,

59

eye stones (the stones of heart's joy) lay on her lap in abundance.

Yet barely the lament about her brother had reached her ears than Belili scattered the jewellery covering her body,

her eye stones (fell down and) now filled the *front of the stool*.

(Belili:) 'My only brother you may not take away from me by force!'

(Belili/Ishtar:) 'During the days on which Dumuzi ascends for my sake, on which the one with the lapis lazuli flute and the one with the carnelian ring ascends for my sake,

on which the male and female mourner ascend with him for my sake,

the dead may ascend and may they smell the incense!'

The Ishtar Hymn of Ammiditana

Michael P. Streck

Extol the goddess, the awe-inspiring among the goddesses!

Praised be the mistress of mankind, the greatest among the Igigi gods.

Extol Ishtar, the awe-inspiring among the goddesses!

Praised be the mistress of womankind, the greatest among the Igigi gods.

She, full of joy, is vested in charm.

Attired she is in seductive appearance, cosmetics and attractiveness.

Ishtar, full of joy, is vested in charm.

Attired she is in seductive appearance, cosmetics and attractiveness.

With sweet lips her mouth is life.

Who looks upon her features, laughter burgeons inside him.

She is splendid. Jewels are placed on her head.

Her complexion is fair and beautiful. Radiant and sparkling are her eyes.

The goddess – good advice is found with her.

She holds the fates of all in her hands.

Under her gaze prosperity comes into being,

dignity, splendour, protection and safeguard.

Over love, obedience, passion, benevolence

and harmony she alone is ruling.

A girl who …, will find a mother (in her).

It is spoken to her among the *people/women*, her name is mentioned.

Who is it? Who is her equal in greatness?

Strong, exalted, paramount are her divine powers.

Ishtar – who is her equal in greatness?

Strong, exalted, paramount are her divine powers.

She is the *spokeswoman* among the gods. Her position is outstanding.

Her word carries weight. She is mightier than them (the gods).

Ishtar – her position is outstanding among the gods.

Her word carries weight. She is mightier than them.

They are mindful of the orders of their queen.

They all kneel before her.

They head for her light.

Women and men worship her.

In their (the gods') council her speech is princely, powerful.

She sits among them *with equal rank* as Anum, their king.

She is wise, (provided) with insight, wisdom and reason.

She and her/their ruler confer with each other.

Together they sit on the throne.

In the temple, the residence of exultation,

the gods stand before them.

Attentively they wait for their/her speech.

The king, her protégé, favourite of her heart is in the splendid habit to present to them his pure offering.

Ammiditana *makes* the pure offering from his hands

splendidly before them: fat bulls and rams.

From Anum, her husband, she requested for him (the king)

a long eternal life.

Many years in life

gave and gifted Ishtar to Ammiditana.

On her behest she brought

the four corners of the world under his feet

and the entire inhabited earth

she placed under his yoke.

Her heart's desire, the song of her beauty,

befit his (the king's) mouth. The words of the god Ea he carried out for her.

He (Ea) heard her praise and rejoiced about him (the king):

'May he live. May his king (the god Marduk?) love him forever.'

Oh Ishtar, give Ammiditana, the king who loves you,

a long eternal life!

May he live!

His antiphon.

Enheduana Sings Against the Imminent Destruction. A Sumerian Song for a Dangerous Ritual by the Earliest Female Author of World Literature

Annette Zgoll

Mistress of the innumerate divine powers, light which has risen radiantly,

woman full of mighty deeds, in the blinding glamour of terror, bound in love to the celestial god An and earth goddess Urash,

ruler over the sky, owner of all great insignia of dominion (on earth),

who loves the potent tiara which she has made fit for the pontifical office,

mighty in the possession of the seven divine powers of high priesthood!

My lady! You are the guardian of the great divine powers!

These powers you have lifted up to your side, these powers you have grasped firmly.

These powers you have brought together all, these powers you have squeezed tightly to yourself.

Like a dragon you have flung poison onto the enemy land!

Where you have roared thunderously like the storm god Ishkur, the grain goddess Ezinam (and thus the harvest) has gone because of you.

Flood of water tumbling down from above onto such a hostile land,

the highest in rank, of sky and earth you are the Inana!

Fire, rekindled anew again and again, spattered down onto the land of Sumer,

whom An has given the divine powers, mistress hastening along on beasts of prey,

who executes An's word, determining fate by her word:

all your great rituals securing the rule – who knows them?

Destroyer of the enemy countries – to the raging of the storm you have given strength.

In loving agreement with Enlil you have let terrible horrors burden the land of Sumer.

To carry out the instructions of An you are standing at the ready.

My lady! When all hostile lands bow before your outcry of war,

after the men hurried (stupefied) to you in terrified silence before the terrible dismay, the blinding glamour and the howling storm,

– you had indeed seized the most terrible of the divine powers –

then the threshold of tears had been passed because of you,

then they began to take the path to the house of great lament towards you;

capitulating because of you, bare of all weapons.

My lady, what strength is yours! When it squashes the hardest material (i.e. flint or teeth),

when you drive in – ceaselessly spitting – like the incessantly hissing raging of the storm,

when you hit – ceaselessly rampaging – with the incessantly riotous raging of the storm,

– with the storm god Ishkur you are roaring thunderously –

when you spend yourself relentlessly raging in grim storms, implacable thunderstorms, wherein you yourself know no fatigue,

then they intone the lamentation with the wailing harp:

my lady! Then the Anuna, the great gods, have fluttered up like jolted bats because of you to hide themselves in the cracks of the mounds of ruins.

Your ghastly gaze they have not withstood,

your gruesome brow none of them can defy.

Your heart glowing in anger – who will cool it down calmingly?

To calm your heart when filled with grim plans is an enormous task!

Lady, is the temper already appeased? Lady, is heart already joyous again?

If you are still furious, heart and temper will not cool down calmly for you, great daughter of Suen!

Lady superior to every enemy land – who could ever withdraw something (unpunished) from your territory?

When you incorporate a 'mountain chain' into your territory, then the grain goddess Ezinam is wholly denied to it (i.e. then there is nothing to eat available in this city).

To its great gates fire was set.

In its canals blood ran because of you, its people had nothing else to drink.

All its troops they had to lead before you.

All their elite units they had to disband for you.

All their vigorous men they have placed before you.

Into the places of entertainment of their city the raging of the storm entered.

Their best men they chased in fetters to you.

When a city did not say: 'The land (belongs) to you!',

when the people did not say; 'He (the city god) is your father!',

then he has spoken your fate-determining word and the place is subjugated to you.

Then there cannot grow any new life in its wombs.

The woman there – with her husband she no longer speaks lovingly.

At night she no longer cultivates council with him.

Her body containing the hope for future life she no longer bares for him there.

Attacking wild cow, great daughter of Suen,

lady superior to the sky – who could ever withdraw anything (unpunished) from your territory?

Great lady (nin gal) of the ladies! For the potent divine powers having emerged from the fated womb,

(now) superior to your own mother (Ningal),

wise and far-seeing, mistress of all lands,

who grants life to many men, your fateful song I will now intone for you!

Deity mighty in deeds to whom the divine powers are due, your magnificent disposition is the most powerful!

Woman mighty in deeds, with inscrutable radiant heart, your divine powers I will name you now!

In my fateful part of the temple district (of the city god of Ur) I had joined you,

I, the high priestess, I, Enheduana.

While I carried the basket for a special ritual,

had intoned the festival jubilation,

then the mortuary offerings were set up, as if my own life had already ended!

I came very close to the light: there I became scorchingly hot.

I came very close to the shadow: after it was veiled for me by the raging of a storm (too),

there my sweet sounding mouth became noisome,

all with which I usually caused joy turned to dust.

My fate with Suen and (the usurper) Lugalane report to An! An may resolve it for me!

Now immediately report it to An. An will resolve it for us!

(An's utterance:) 'The fate of Lugalane will be snatched away by a woman.

Because mountains (i.e. enemy countries) and floods of water lie subjugated at her feet,

because this woman is mighty (also faced with other adversaries), she will let the city tremble before her.

Appear (in court) so that she will calm soothingly for me that which is restless in her heart!'

Enheduana am I – a prayer I will now speak to you.

My tearful lament, as if it was a pleasant libation,

I will now let loose before you, Inana, determining the fate, '(It is up to) you to carry out (the) sentence!' I now say to you.

Concerning Dilimbabbar, do not trouble yourself!

During (the disaster that) right up to the rituals of purification of the fate-determining An everything concerning him has been spoiled,

he (Lugalane) has snatched away from An (his temple) Eana!

To the venerable god (An) he has shown no reverence!

This temple of whose delight he (An) had truly never had enough, of whose beauty he would never have tired,

this temple he (Lugalane) has turned into a place of abhorrence for him (An)!

A kind of 'companion' ...! – While he had joined me in that manner, he has come to me (in truth) with his envy!

My mighty divine wild cow! Him you shall chase away, him you shall seize!

In the place enabling life – I – what am I there now?

As a rebelling region hateful to your Nanna, An shall hand it (Ur) over!

This city – An shall smite it!

Enlil shall curse it!

No mother shall soothe a crying child of this city (and that means, too: no city goddess shall calm her lamenting protégé)!

Lady! That which has aroused lamentation,

namely your 'ship of laments', shall be left behind in enemy territory!

Or do I have to die, because I have intoned my song determining fate?

Concerning me – my Nanna has not asked after me,

when the renegade region destroyed me bones and all.

Dilimbabbar has most certainly not passed judgement on me!

If he has passed it or not – what has to be done now?

After he (Dilimbabbar or Lugalane) has achieved all his desires triumphantly, he has let it (the judgement) come forth from the temple.

Like a swallow he has shooed me from the window. After he has ensured that the people have demolished my life,

you (Inana) let it happen that I now have to go into the thorny thicket of the enemy land?

The potent tiara of the pontifical office he snatched away from me,

gave me a dagger and said: 'This is now your jewellery!'

Unique lady beloved by An,

your fate-determining heart is enormous(ly furious):

May it return for my sake (to its territory)!

Spouse who loves the (legitimate ruler) Ushumgalana!

From the foundations of the sky to its zenith you are the great lady (nin gal),

the elevated gods, the Anuna, have bowed down to you.

From birth you were the smaller mistress,

but now that you have surpassed the Anuna, all the great gods,

they kiss with their lips the ground before you.

Although my own trial is not yet concluded, I am surrounded by a foreign, hostile judgement as if it were destined for me.

The radiantly pure bed he (Lugalane) had not soiled,

the spells of (the city goddess) Ningal I have not revealed to that wretch.

The radiant En priestess of Nanna am I.

My lady, beloved of An, may your heart cool down for me in calmness!

It shall be known, it shall be known: Nanna has passed no sentence, 'It is yours', he has said!

That you are mightily high as the sky shall be known!

That you are immeasurably wide as the earth shall be known!

That you annihilate the renegade regions shall be known!

That you roar against enemy lands shall be known!

That you smite the heads (of the rebellion) shall be known!

That you eat (their) carcasses like an animal of prey shall be known!

That your gaze brings grisly ruin shall be known!

That you will employ this gaze of terror shall be known!

That your gaze radiates a destructive blaze everywhere shall be known!

That you are imperturbable and unyielding shall be known!

That you achieve all your desires triumphantly shall be known!

That Nanna has passed no sentence, that he has said 'It is yours', that has made you even greater, my lady, you are the mightiest of all –

and therefore, you my lady, whom An loves, I will tell herewith of all your irresistible raging!

The coals I have heaped up, the rituals of purification prepared for it,

the temple Eshdamku ('fate-determining shelter') is ready for you: will your heart not cool down calmly for my sake?

As my heart had become full, as it had become overflowing,

mighty mistress, I have created this for you.

What was said to you during the night,

shall the ritual singer repeat for your at noon:

'After your anger had become great because of your captured spouse, because of your captured protégée, then your heard could not find rest …!'

The mighty mistress, the ruler of the (gods') assembly,

she has accepted the ritual of her.

The heart of the fate-determining Inana has turned to its/his territory for her sake.

The day was pleasant for her, she spread rapture, she exuded profuse beauty in abundance.

Like the risen moonlight (Nanna) she dressed herself in radiant beauty.

Nanna expressed his admiration energetically,

she (Inana) greeted her mother Ningal,

and while the gate keeper deities offer their welcome to her (Inana)

that, which she (Ningal) apportions to the mistress, is enormous!

The destroyer of all enemy lands, who has received the divine powers from An,

my lady, draped in delight, to you, Inana, belongs this song of praise!

King Utuhengal Expels the Gutians

Walther Sallaberger

Enlil – Gutium, the snake and scorpion vermin of the mountains, the rowdy against the gods, who carried away Sumer's kingship into the mountainside, who filled Sumer with evil, who took from the one, who had a wife, the wife for himself, who took from the one, who had a child, the child for himself, who established evil and violence throughout the land, –

Enlil, the king of the countries, he had to destroy his (=Gutium's) name for Utuhengal, the strong, the man of Uruk, the king of the four corners of the world, he, the king against whose dictum they cannot turn, he, Enlil, the lord of the lands, has commissioned him with this.

With Inana, his lady, he entered. He prayed to her. 'My lady, lioness of the battle, who fights with the lands, Enlil has commissioned me to restore the kingship of Sumer, be my helpmate!'

The army of the foreigners has settled there. Tirigan, the king of Gutium, has ordered it and nobody appeared against him. He occupied the Tigris on both banks. Towards the lower end in Sumer he blocked the fields, towards the upper end he blocked the paths, on the routes through the land he let the grass grow long.

The king, gifted by Enlil with strength, whom Inanna has called into the (pure) heart, Utuhengal, the strong man, came from Uruk to meet

76

him. In (the place) House of Ishkur he drove in the stakes (for the camp), to the sons of his city he spoke: 'Gutium was given to me by Enlil, my lady Inana is my helpmate, (god) Dumuzi-ama'ushumgal'ana has declared it mine, Gilgamesh, Ninsumun's son, he has given to me as advocate.'

With this he brought joy to the sons of Uruk and Kulaba: like a single man they followed him! A look at his elite unit, then he put them into march formation. On the fourth day after his departure from (the place) House of Ishkur he erected a camp in Kabsu at the Iturungal [river]. On the fifth day he made camp in Ili-tappe.

Ur-Ninazu and Nabi-Enlil, the generals of Tirigan, who carried a message to Sumer, he (Utuhengal) seized and clapped their hands in irons.

On the sixth day after his departure from Ili-tappe he erected his camp at the entrance to Karkar. There he stepped up to the weather god Ishkur and prayed to him. 'Ishkur, Enlil has given me the weapon, be my helpmate!'

Before dawn he decamped. Above, opposite of Adab, he stepped before the rising sun and prayed: 'Sun god Utu, Gutium, this has Enlil given to me, be my helpmate!'

At this place, the front (of) Gutium, there *he opened battle with him*. The troops he led towards him. Utuhengal, the strong man, won here.

On this day Tirigan, the king of Gutium, stole away on foot all by himself. There whereto he had saved his life, in Dabrum, there it was good for him. Yet because the people of Dabrum knew that Utuhengal is the king to whom Enlil had given the power, they did not let Tirigan go.

Utuhengal's messenger seized Tirigan and his wife and children in Dabrum, clapped his hand in irons, [and] covered his eyes with a cloth.

Utuhengal has placed him before the sun god Utu at his feet, he has placed his foot onto his neck. Gutium, the dagger snake of the mountains, … .

The kingship of Sumer he brought back into his hand again.

Gilgamesh and Akka

Hans Neumann

Messengers of Akka, the son of Emmebaragesi, came from Kish to Gilgamesh in Uruk. In front of the elders of the city Gilgamesh presented the matter, looking for council: 'The wells have to be completed, all wells of the land (Sumer) have to be completed, all the shallow wells of the land (Sumer) have to be completed, all the deep wells (with) hoisting ropes have to be completed – we should not submit to the house of Kish, we want to beat it at arms!' In the assembly convened from the elders of his city Gilgamesh was answered: 'The wells have to be completed, all wells of the land (Sumer) have to be completed, all the shallow wells of the land (Sumer) have to be completed, all the deep wells (with) hoisting ropes have to be completed – to the house of Kish we want to submit, we do not wish to beat it at arms!'

Gilgamesh, the lord of Kulaba, who trusts in (the goddess) Inana, (however,) did not take the words of the elders of his city to heart. A second time, (now) in front of the able-bodied men of his town, Gilgamesh presented the matter, looking for council: 'The wells have to be completed, all wells of the land (Sumer) have to be completed, all the shallow wells of the land (Sumer) have to be completed, all the deep wells (with) hoisting ropes have to be completed – we should not submit to the house of Kish, we want to beat it at arms!' In the assembly convened from the able-bodied men of his city Gilgamesh was answered: 'As it is said (in the proverb): 'Always to be ready for duty and present, to accompany the son of the king, to always take the reins of the donkey – who has the necessary breath (for this)?' We should not submit to the house of Kish, we want to beat it at arms! From Uruk – the handiwork of the gods, from the temple E'ana – descended from the sky, whose structure the great gods have created. Over its great wall which touches the ground (like) a bank of fog, over the lofty residence founded by (the celestial god) An, you have stood watch – you are its king (and) hero! Oh *batterer of heads,* prince beloved of An, if he (Akka) comes – how will he have to be afraid! His army is small, disorganised in the rearguard, his men are incapable to withstand a confrontation!'

Thereupon the heart of Gilgamesh, the lord of Kubala, was gladdened by the words of the able-bodied men of his city, his disposition became cheerful. To his servant Enkidu he spoke: 'Now then, let the equipment and the weapons for battle be prepared! Let the mace return to your side! Let it create great horror (and) blaze of terror! If he (Akka) comes, (the) great terror (caused by) me shall overcome him! His senses shall be confused, his (power of) judgement shall be impaired!' Neither five nor ten days had (passed, when) Akka, the son of Enmebaragesi, surrounded Uruk (with his troops). The mind of Uruk was confused.

Gilgamesh, the lord of Kulaba, spoke to his warriors: 'My warriors look concerned! A brave man may step forward (and say): 'To Akka I will go!' Birkhurtura, his royal *bodyguard,* spoke full of enthusiasm to his king: 'My king, I will go to Akka! His (Akka's) senses may be confused, his (power of judgement) may be impaired!' Birkhurtura went out of the city gate. When Birkhurtura exited the city gate, they (= the men of Akka) seized him at the entrance of the gate, they beat Birkhurtura from head to toe. (Then) they brought him before Akka. (Thereupon) he directed the word at Akka, but before he finished his speech, the 'cup bearer' of Uruk climbed upon the wall (of the city) (and) leaned over the wall. Akka saw him (and) spoke to Birkhurtura: 'Slave, is this man there your king?' 'This man there is not my king. If this man there was my king, (then) it would be his angry forehead, his eye of the wisent, his beard of lapis lazuli, his beneficial fingers. Would not then multitudes fall, multitudes rise, would not multitudes mingle with the sand, would then not all foreign lands be overpowered, would not the mouth of the land be filled with dust, would not the horns (= stems) of the barges be torn off, would he then not take captive Akka, the king of Kish, amidst his own troops?' (Thereupon) they pummelled him, they beat him. Birkhurtura they beat from head to toe.

After the 'cup bearer' of Uruk Gilgamesh ascended the wall, his aura overpowered old and young of Kubala. The able-bodied men of Uruk armed themselves with maces (and) arrayed themselves along the road by the city gate. (Thereafter) Enkidu emerged from the city gate alone (and) Gilgamesh leaned over the wall. Glancing upwards Akka caught sight of him (and spoke to Enkidu): 'Slave, is that man there your king?' (Enkidu answered:) 'This man there is my king!'. It was as he (Birkhurtura) had said: multitudes fell, multitudes rose, multitudes mingled with dust, all foreign lands were overpowered, the mouth of the land was filled with dust, the horns (stems) of the barges were torn off, Akka, the king of Kish, he took captive amidst his own troops. ...

Gilgamesh, the lord of Kubala, spoke to Akka: 'Oh Akka, my lieutenant, Akka, my captain – oh Akka, my prince of the city, Akka, my general! Oh Akka, my commander of troops! Akka, breath of life you have given to me, Akka, life you have given to me: Akka, you have protected the refugee in your lap, Akka, you have nurtured the fleeing bird with barley. Uruk, the handiwork of the gods – over its great wall touching the ground (like) a bank of fog, over its lofty residence founded by An I have held watch – reward (yourself) now for the good deed done to me. Before (the sun god) Utu I repay you herewith the blessing of the past!' Akka he let go free to Kish.

Oh Gilgamesh, lord of Kulaba, your praise is sweet!

Birth and Rise of King Sargon

Sabina Franke

Sargon, the strong king, the king of Akkade, am I. My mother was a high priestess, my father I do not know. My paternal family lived in the mountainside. My birth place is Azupiranu located on the Euphrates. My mother, the high priestess, conceived and gave birth to me in secrecy. She placed me into a willow basket and sealed it with bitumen. She abandoned me on the river from where I could not escape. The river carried me away. To Aqqi, the water carrier, it brought me, when he dipped in his bailer. Aqqi, the water carrier, brought me up as his son. Aqqi, the water carrier, instructed me in his gardening duties. During my gardening the goddess Ishtar grew fond of me so that I reigned *55 years as king*. I ruled and reigned over the black-headed people. I … difficult mountains with copper rods. Mountain tops I climbed up again and again, over hills I jumped again and again. The marshland I lay siege to three times, *conquered* Dilmun … . I *marched* to the great walls of sky and earth …, I … . I destroyed … . Whatever king rules after me: *he shall also reign 55 years as king*. He shall *reign* and (also) *rule over* the black-headed people. He shall … difficult mountains with copper *rods*. He shall climb mountain tops again and again, too. *He shall jump over hills again and again.* He shall also lay siege to the marshland three times. *He shall conquer Dilmun, too … . He shall also* march *to the great walls of sky and earth* … from my city Akkade … .

(The end of the text is not preserved.)

A Dialogue About the Indifference of the Gods: the Babylonian Theodicy

Hannelore Agnethler / Marc Elsässer

(The sufferer)

Wise one, … , now then, I will give account to you.

… will I tell you.

…

I who is suffering terribly will praise you forever.

Where is there an insightful [man] who is on a par with you?

Where is found a wise man who is comparable to you?

Where is the advisor to whom I could present my woe?

I was destroyed, tribulations lay ahead of me.

I am a late arrival, my father was snatched away by fate.

The mother who had borne me went back to the land without return.

My father and my mother left me behind, a tutor I did not have.

(The friend)

Dear friend, what you have spoken is dismal.

My dear, who have let your mind seek evil,

your acute intellect you made like that of an impotent,

your radiant face you have let become dark.

Our fathers are surrendered *to death* and walk the pass of death.

The river Hubur has to be crossed, so it is destined since time immemorial.

You see mankind, as a whole, the *mortals*:

the heir of the pauper has ascended, has anyone made him rich?

Diligent is the owner of wealth, who has done him good?

Who looks upon the face of god finds vigour.

The hard-pressed fearing the goddess accumulates abundance.

(The sufferer)

A spring, friend, is your heart, whose waters do not run dry,

a vast ocean whose volume knows no diminution.

Now I want to ask you a question, learn of my concern!

Be attentive now, hear my words!

Shrouded is my figure, hardship dulls me.

My success has vanished, lost is my surplus.

My strengths have slackened, my gain is at its end.

Melancholy and sorrow blacken my face.

The rations of my meadows do not suffice to satisfy me.

The beer, the food of men, does not sate my hunger.

Are better days intended for me? I would like to know.

(The friend)

Oh my [friend] who speaks aptly, mountain ... !

Your ordered mind *you pervert* to confused talking.

Distractedly and thoughtlessly you approach ... .

Like an indecisive *you made* your chosen ... .

Constantly and without pause ... that which you desire.

The one giving protection ... through prayer.

The forgiving goddess returns to ... .

Him ..., who is not orderly they show mercy ... .

The just ritual order seek out constantly!

The strong ... may grant assistance!

... may bestow mercy!

(The sufferer)

I have bowed down before you, I have taken in your advice.

... the utterance *of your words*.

... now then, I will give account to you.

The wild donkey, the onager, which has sated itself on …, does its mind actually rest upon the execution of the divine calculation?

The wild lion which always eats the choice cuts of meat,

did it actually make its offering of flour in order to placate the goddess' fury?

… the parvenu whose wealth has multiplied, has he actually weighed out precious gold for the goddess Mami?

Have I held back offerings? To the gods I have prayed.

The regular offerings to the goddess I have made, my word … .

(The friend)

Oh date palm, tree of wealth, my precious brother!

Boon of all wisdom, jewel of … !

You are a child of the earth, far is the council of god.

Observe the magnificent onager in the steppe!

The rooter which tramples the fields is persecuted by the arrow.

The enemy of the cattle, the lion, now then, this what you mention, observe closely!

The injustice committed by the lion, (for this) the pit has been opened for it.

The one gifted with wealth, the parvenu amassing possessions,

in the fire, long before his time, the king will burn him.

The path which these have followed do you wish to tread?

Aspire after god's reward constantly!

(The sufferer)

A northern wind is your mind, a pleasant breeze for mankind.

Distinguished friend, your advice is sound.

Only one word I wish to add.

A good path is trodden by those who do not follow god.

Poor and weak become those who plead devoutly with the goddess.

In my youth I strove after the will of god.

By supplication and pious prayer I sought my goddess.

The futile duty I bore constantly like a yoke.

(Yet) god determined, instead of riches, poverty.

Above me is a cripple, before me an idiot.

Ruffians rose, but I was debased.

(The friend)

Oh unyielding [man] who was granted wisdom, your considerations are foolish.

The virtue you have discarded, the plan of the gods you dismiss.

Not to maintain the divine rituals you verily wish in your heart.

The enduring cults of the goddess … .

Like the innermost place of the sky the intentions of the gods *are hidden* … .

The order of the goddess can*not be ripped* from her mouth … .

Firm is the understanding ... .

Their efforts for mankind ... .

The vicissitude of the goddess *they comprehend* ... .

Nigh is their planning ... .

...

(The sufferer)

...

(The friend)

...

(The sufferer)

...

(The friend)

...

(The sufferer)

The house I will abandon ... .

Possession I will not covet ... .

The god's cults I will neglect, the customs I will treat with contempt.

The young bull I will kill, I will eat ... .

Away I will go to visit the yonder.

A well I will open, a flood [I will] unleash.

Between the fields I will wander around like a thief.

From house to house I will go, will sate my hunger.

Hungrily I will rove about, through the alleyways I will roam.

Miserable … .

Far away *is* the good … .

(The friend)

…

(The sufferer)

…

… says the daughter to the mother.

Fallen has the bird catcher who cast *his net*.

Whoever it may be, … the success … .

Numerous is the wildlife of the steppe which … .

Is there one among them who receives … .

Son and daughter I will search for … .

What I find may not leave *me* … .

(The friend)

…

(The sufferer)

…

The son of a king dresses himself … .

The son of a pauper and naked man is dressed … .

The guardian of the malt … gold.

Who weighs out red (gold), carries … .

Who (usually) eats greens, *eats* a prince's meal.

The son of the mighty and rich lives off carob beans.

Fallen is the owner of riches, far is … .

(The friend)

…

A law since time immemorial are wealth and poverty.

(The sufferer)

… the insight.

You possess all wisdom, the people you advise.

… *the death* far?

… of the bird catcher they bring.

… my heart *does not stop*.

… *seize* my lips.

… my stylus.

… its/his inscription he revealed to me.

… revealed his face to me.

Certainly the destruction of my happiness is very near.

... I flash around.

(The friend)

...

in a flurry you put your sensitive heart.

... the wisdom you have driven out.

Decency you have rejected, the laws you have disobeyed.

... far the hamper.

... is made a powerful man.

... is called knowledgeable.

His head is held high, he receives what he desires.

Follow the order of the gods, preserve their cults!

... and be virtuous!

(The sufferer)

...

(The friend)

...

Concerning the scoundrel whose favour you crave,

... of his legs will soon vanish.

The godless, the villain, receives possessions,

(yet) the killing of his weapon torments him.

You who do not seek the plan of the gods, what is your gain?

Who strains under god's yoke, may be scrawny, (but) his food arrives regularly.

Always search for the refreshing breeze of the gods,

what you have lost in a year, you will replace in no time!

(The sufferer)

Among mankind I have looked around, the circumstances are different.

God does not thwart the plans of the Sharrabu demon.

On the river the father drags the ship,

(and) in the bed lies sleeping his firstborn.

Like a lion the oldest brother walks his path,

(and) the younger (already) rejoices, when he leads a mule.

The heir roams the streets like a vagabond,

(and) the younger brother gives sustenance to the needy.

I who prostrated myself before the gods, what advantage do I have?

(Even) among the lowest I kneel.

Disdainfully the riffraff looks at me, (just like) the rich and the proud.

(The friend)

Diligent, knowledgeable, master of wit,

your heart is very bad, and now you are beleaguering god.

The mind of god is as far removed as the interior of the sky.

His power is difficult to understand, men do not grasp it.

Among all creatures by the hand of Aruru, among everything alive,

the first offspring has not entirely broken away.

The cow, its first calf is meagre,

its later young the double of it.

The stupid son is born first,

diligent and brave, so the second is called.

They may watch out for that which is the will of the gods,

(but) men do not know it.

(The sufferer)

Be vigilant, my friend, realise my intentions!

Retain the eminent statement of my words.

They venerate the words of the mighty familiar with murder.

They disregard the *one without possessions* who is not to blame.

They support the unscrupulous for whom decency is an anathema.

They expel the upright who honours god's plan.

They fill with gold the hoard of the evildoer.

They empty the storage jars which are the rations of the needy.

They encourage the superior in whom all is rotten.

The feeble-minded they destroy, they edge away the incapable.

And me, the wretched, me torments the parvenu.

(The friend)

The king of gods, Narru, who created the *mortals*,

the splendid Zulummaru who lifted up their loam,

the queen who formed them, the lady Mami.

They gave the confused speech to mankind.

With lies and not with honesty they endowed them for eternity.

They solemnly praise the rich:

he is a king, riches are on his side!

Like a thief men abuse the *one without possessions*.

They heap spite upon him, they plan his murder.

Maliciously they burden him with all evils because he is lacking *leadership*.

Spiritless they let him collapse and extinguish him like embers.

(The sufferer)

You are merciful, my friend, hear my lament!

Help me! I have seen suffering. Understand:

a servant, wise and pious, am I.

Help and support I did not see for a moment.

Calmly I crossed the plaza of my city.

My voice did not rise, hushed was my speech.

My head I did not raise, my gaze I kept lowered.

Like a servant I sing no praise in the company of my fellows.

Help may be given by the god who has abandoned me.

Mercy may be mustered by the goddess who ... .

The shepherd, the sun of mankind, *may* like a god ... .

From the Life of a Student

Karin Stella Schmidt

'Student, where did you go for so long?' – 'To the Edubba'a I went!' –

'What did you do in the Edubba'a?' –

'My clay tablet I have read, my school breakfast I have eaten, have prepared, have written and completed my tablet (for writing). (Then) they let me write (copy) my prescribed lines, afterwards they assigned me a hand tablet (as text exercise). After the end (of the lessons) in the Edubba'a I went home. I entered the house, my father was sitting (there). I recited my hand tablet to my father, my father was satisfied (with me).

I placed myself before my father: 'I am thirsty – give (me) water to drink! I am hungry – give (me) bread! Wash my feet, prepare my bed, I wish to lie down!', I said (to him). 'Wake me in the morning, I do not wish to waste time, (otherwise) my (teaching) master will beat me!' When I rose early in the morning, I turned to my mother: 'Give (me) my breakfast, I wish to go to the Edubba'a', I said to her. When my mother had given me two loaves of bread, … before *her eyes*. When my mother had given me two (further) loaves of bread, I went to the Edubba'a.

In the Edubba'a the man on duty said to me: 'Why have you wasted time?' I became scared, my heart palpitated. I stepped up to my master and bowed low. My Edubba'a father read my clay tablet: 'Because you missed out a line' (he said), (for this) he beat me. When the supervisors said that it was break time, ... the school breakfast. When the master was about to check the code of conduct of the Edubba'a, the one responsible for ... said: 'On the street you have looked around, ... *your garment not donned properly*!', he beat me. My Edubba'a father placed my clay tablet before me. The man of the court said: 'Write!' I immediately set down at my place. My clay tablet I had at hand, the template lay directly in front (of me). I wrote my clay tablet and *fulfilled my tasks*. Without being asked, my mouth formed words soundlessly in doing so. The one responsible for keeping the silence said: 'Why do you speak without my permission?', he beat me. The one responsible for *manners* said: 'Why have you not seated yourself erectly?', he beat me. The one responsible for maintaining the rules (said): 'Why did you stand up without my permission?', he beat me. The porter (said): 'Why did you go out without my permission?', he beat me. The one responsible for the jar (said): 'Why have you taken *water* without my permission?', he beat me. The Sumerian teacher (said): '*Akkadian* have you spoken', he beat me. My master said: 'Your hand (writing) is entirely unreadable', he beat me. Of the art of writing I had tired (now), ...'

'The master has had no success with you any longer.' – 'In the art of writing ... his strength ... . (As far as) the basic teaching contents of writing and as far as the duties as a Sheshgal in the Edubba'a nothing has ... me.' – 'Give him (the master) his present! The multiplication he shall let you demonstrate. Calculus and accounting he shall leave aside.' – 'From the teaching texts existing in the Edubba'a read by every student I will read aloud, too.'

His father agreed to that which the student has said to this. The master was brought from the Edubba'a. When he had let him enter the house, he let him sit in the place of honour. The student bowed, stood (ready for duty) before him, (everything) he had learned about the art of writing he presented to his father.

97

Out of innermost joy his father spoke before the Edubba'a father of his son: 'My little one, he has offered you much, he has let you become clever. In the art of writing he lets you strive after perfection! (Since) you have shown him the solutions for the contents of the clay tablets, calculus and accounting, you could explain to him all difficult passages of the script.

Let him be poured ..., as if it was good beer, put a table before him! Good oil I will pour him like water over his back and upper body, in a robe I will garb him, give him something, put a ring/circlet on his hand!'

He let him be poured ..., as if it was good beer, the table he put before him. Like water he poured fragrant oil over his back and upper body, he garbed him in a robe, he gave him something, put a ring/circlet on his hand.

The master blessed him from his innermost joy: 'Young man, who you have taken heed of my word(s) and not neglected them, you have not baulked in any manner – following the high art of writing, perfecting (it) until its goal –, so you have presented it to me! He (the father) surpassed my effort by giving a gift: by him is (thus) something special added. Nisaba, the lady of the tutelary deities, may be your patron goddess! She may direct your good stylus forever positively for you, she may let you find errors in (each) hand tablet available to you! For your brothers may you be a model, (among) your friends may you be the best, and an example for the students may you be! The royal palace *(to visit?) regularly*, ...

Young man, your father knows this: I, (yes) I am the one who follows your father (in importance). The blessing which I granted you, and what I decided for you – therein your god and your father may support you. To your lady Nisaba he will pray like to your own deity, present offerings to her and plead (with her). The master may bless you like your own father! So the hand which you have used for the most magnificent [deed] may affect for you good things (again and again) at the … of the master and of the forehead of the Sheshgal for ever and ever (with) your subordinates. The teachings of the Edubba'a you have realised splendidly, young man, you have become knowledgeable!'

He has proclaimed Nisaba's greatness, the mistress of (the places of) learning, Nisaba be praised!

Bibliography

General bibliography on history, culture and literature
Podany, A.H., *The Ancient Near East*, Oxford, 2014
Postgate, J.N., *Early Mesopotamia*, Routledge, London & New York, 1994
Roaf, M., *A Cultural Atlas of Mesopotamia*, 1990
Snell, D.C., *A Companion to the Ancient Near East*, Blackwell 2007

Translations
Foster, B.R., *Before the Muses*, Bethesda, 2003, contains an extensive anthology of Akkadian literature. The translations from the web pages http://etcsl.orinst.ox.ac.uk (Sumerian literature) and http://www.etana.org/etact (selected Akkadian literature) are as a rule more literal and have additional notes. In the following translations from these publications are not referred to specifically. For both Sumerian and Akkadian literature and texts visit the Open Richly Annotated Cuneiform Corpus http://oracc.museum.upenn.edu/.

Notes on the texts

When the gods were human

The myth of Atramhasis tells the history of mankind from its creation until the Great Flood, in which only the family of Atramhasis – labelled as 'exceedingly wise' by his name – is spared by the disaster. Known through more than twenty manuscripts in the Akkadian language, the passing on of this work from the so-called Old Babylonian Period until the Neo-Babylonian Period demonstrates its great popularity. The earliest version, presented here, from the reign of King Ammi-aduqa (17th century BC), ran to 1,245 lines, of which roughly two-thirds are preserved today.

The myth begins before mankind's creation, 'when the gods were human', and were themselves responsible for their provisioning. Triggered by a rebellion of the working Igigu gods, the great ruling Anunaku gods decide on the advice of the god of wisdom Ea (Sumerian Enki) to create men for the 'service of the gods'. Mankind's creation happens as a collaboration of Ea and the mother goddess Belet-ili (alias Mami or Nintu). They create, from the flesh and blood of the god We, who instigated the rebellion, mixed with loam, the primordial man who owes his immortal spirit to his divine component. Quickly men multiply, becoming a raucous people whom Enlil, the principal god on earth, seeks to decimate by three kinds of plague: epidemic, drought and famine. Each time Ea helps men created by him to avert the plague by giving pertinent instructions to his particularly pious devotee Atramhasis. Even when Enlil sends the ultimate disaster in form of the deluge, Ea, banned from communications, manages to warn his protégé Atramhasis by a ruse and supply him with the life-saving instruction to build an ark. Finally almost the whole of mankind is eradicated by the deluge, as a result of which the cult of the gods grinds to a halt. After the rescue of Atramhasis and once his renewed offerings to the gods have been accepted, the gods hold council on how the growth of mankind could be regulated in future, namely by female infertility, infant mortality and religious celibacy.

Lambert, W.G./Millard, A.R., *Atra-hasîs. The Babylonian Story of the Flood*, Oxford 1969

Shehata, D., *Annotierte Bibliographie zum altbabylonischen Atramhasis-Mythos*, Göttingen 2001

The tooth worm

Toothache has existed, according to this invocation, since the creation of the world. Just as fruits become rotten and worm-eaten with time, teeth also rot due to the tooth worm sitting within the gums. The invocation was an attempt to drive out the worm and stop the pain.

Thompson, R.C., *Cuneiform Texts vol. 17*, p50, London 1903

Hecker, K., *Untersuchungen zur Akkadischen Epik, Alter Orient und Altes Testament S 8*, Kevelaer/Neukirchen/Vluyn 1974, p3–5

Hubmann, A., *Der Zahnwurm. Die Geschichte eines volksheilkundlichen Glaubens*, Regensburg 2008

Letter of request to a god

The small clay tablet originates from the antiquities market and can be dated to the Old Babylonian Period. A desperate man not only pleads with his personal god, but also asks him above all to put in a good word for him with the ruler of the gods, Marduk. It becomes very clear that the relationship between god and man is one of give and take, as the praying man threatens the god with the withdrawal of offerings if he receives no help. The letter was probably deposited in the temple, as a lasting reminder to the god.

Lutz, H., *Yale Oriental Studies 2*, New Haven 1917, no. 141

Stol, M., *Altbabylonische Briefe 9*, Leiden 1981, 89–91

Lullaby

The plight of sleepless infants' mothers is emphatically visualised in this invocation. The Akkadian text dates to the Old Babylonian Period (*c.*1900–1600 BC) and is found on a clay tablet with several invocations for the protection of children.

Farber, W., *Schlaf, Kindchen, Schlaf!*, *Mesopotamian Civilizations*, Winona Lake 1989, p34–35

The master and his servant

The dialogue composed in Akkadian (also known as 'Pessimistic Dialogue') is found in copies from the 1st millennium BC from the sites of Assur, Nineveh and Babylon. It is structured in ten stanzas of the same layout. A protagonist called 'master' lets an antagonist called 'servant' invent answers to different aspects of Mesopotamian daily life. Herein each aspect is scrutinised first by the positive side, then by the negative one. This stereotypically designed game of questions and answers results in contrasts and contradictions which partly deviate from the norms valid in Assyria and Babylonia. The dialogue form of the piece has instructive character. In the statements of the servant are found, among other matters, worldly wisdom, criticism of religion and society, humour and satire.

The partly free German translation is based on the source texts compiled and published in W.G. Lambert, *Babylonian Wisdom Literature*, Oxford 1960, p139–149, p37–38.

The revenge of the poor man from Nippur

This fairytale in Akkadian was found in the library of an exorcist from the 8th/7th century BC in the town of Huzirina close to modern Urfa. It contains not only the successful revenge of a poor man on an arrogant, superior official, but also criticism of various social conditions. Typical for fairytales is the partly missing narrative logic. Similar structure and motifs can be found in fairytales of other cultures.

Gurney, O.R., 'The Sultantepe Tablets V. The Tale of the Poor Man of Nippur', *Anatolian Studies* 6, 1956, p145–164 and *Anatolian Studies* 7, 1957, p135–136

Cooper, J.S., 'Structure, Humor and Satire in The Poor Man of Nippur', *Journal of Cuneiform Studies 27*, 1975, p163–174

Jason, H., 'The Poor Man of Nippur: An Ethnopoetic Analysis', *Journal of Cuneiform Studies 31*, 1979, p189–215

Milano, L., 'Aspects of Meat Consumption in Mesopotamia and the Food Paradigm of the Poor Man of Nippur', *State Archives of Assyria Bulletin 12*, 1998, p111–127

The tale of Etana

The Akkadian narration links a possible historical core with mythical themes and fairytale motifs: the childless Etana seeks the 'herb of childbirth' for his wife in order to have a son. This motif is embedded into prehistoric times, during which the gods designate the city of Kish as the earliest centre of rule and appoint Etana as king there. In order to obtain the herb of childbirth Etana has to rescue an eagle condemned to death from a pit, which in return carries him on his back. The background of the eagle is described in detail; he made friends with a snake, and both swore an oath before the judiciary god Shamash, but the eagle broke the oath by eating the snake's offspring. The snake punishes him by clipping his wings and throwing him into a deep pit. After a longer gap in the text the reader learns how the eagle and Etana reach the goddess Ishtar on divine paths. The end of the text is missing; Etana must, however, have obtained the herb of childbirth, as a son of Etana is known from other sources.

The tale is transmitted fragmentarily, so the given translation takes into consideration only the source texts of the latest of three text versions, as these can be matched with a high probability and are not too heavily fragmented.

The translation presented here is based on published source texts which were most recently compiled by J. Novotny (2001) and supplemented by further original fragments in J. Kinnier Wilson (2007).

Haul, M., *Das Etana-Epos. Ein Mythos von der Himmelfahrt des Königs von Kiš, Göttinger Arbeitshefte zur altorientalischen Literatur*, Göttingen 2000

Novotny, J.R., 'The Standard Babylonian Etana Epic', *State Archives of Assyria Cuneiform Texts II*, Helsinki 2001

Kinnier Wilson, J., 'Studia Etanaica. New Texts and Discussions', *Alter Orient und Altes Testament 338*, Münster 2007

Invitation to the dead for a feast: Ishtar's descent into the world of the dead and Dumuzi's return to the world of the living

This myth is preserved in an earlier Sumerian version (*c.*18th/17th century BC) and in two Akkadian versions. The version from the first half of the 1st millennium BC is well-attested and is found on two tablets from Nineveh and a tablet from Assur, and it is this version that is translated here.

The story describes the descent of the goddess of the morning star (Venus), who possesses power over fertility/love and war, into the underworld and her killing by the powers of the realm of the dead. A member of the Ishtar cult, the Assinnu, manages to please the ruler of the underworld so that she grants him a wish. Ishtar is thus brought back to life. As a replacement she has to surrender her husband Dumuzi to the underworld. Dumuzi's sister Belili alternates with him in the underworld, as other versions describe, so he can leave the realm of the dead regularly. The other dead are allowed back into the world of the living with him. The text is anchored in an important domestic festival to remember the deceased in any family, which was celebrated for three days every year during high summer. The deceased would be dined and honoured. In return the living would expect that the dead, together with Ishtar and Dumuzi, would allow them to continue living. For this purpose Dumuzi is supposed to return the demons of illness, currently walking abroad on the earth, to the underworld.

While the beginning of the text emphasises that the underworld never lets anyone go and that the path to it is a one-way street, the end of the text draws an entirely different picture. The dead are allowed to leave the realm of the dead on certain days and are able to reach the world of the living. That this complete rearrangement of the world can succeed rests upon the plan and deed of Ishtar according to the myth: very clearly, she does not shrink from divesting herself of all instruments of power in order to turn the path to the 'land without return' into a path of return. She herself returns. And her husband is allowed back into the world of the living, at least temporarily. This is an immense achievement: the prison of death is broken open by an act of redemption from this powerful goddess, and the primordial conditions are altered. Thus an essential, deeply significant innovation occurs: mankind is granted – at least once a year –something almost akin to eternal life, while before they lived towards eternal death.

The most recent edition of the text, with bibliography, is found in P. Lapinkivi, *The Neo-Assyrian Myth of Ištar's Descent and Resurrection*, SAACT 6, Helsinki, 2010. The interpretation newly presented here is based on studies by A. Zgoll in the context of the Göttingen collegium mythologicum (http://www.uni-goettingen.de/de/collegium-mythologicum/410971. html).

The Ishtar hymn of Ammiditana

The hymn, consisting of 14 strophes of four verses and a three-line antiphon at the end, praises Ishtar, the goddess of love and sexuality and at the same time one of the most powerful goddesses of the pantheon. The first five strophes describe Ishtar as an attractive woman. The next five strophes discuss her elevated position among the gods. The last four strophes before the antiphon name as 'author' Ammiditana, king of Babylon (*c.*1,683–1,647 BC) who receives his power and a long life from Ishtar.

Thureau-Dangin, F., 'Un hymne à Ištar', *Revue d'Assyriologie 22*, 1925, p169–177

Enheduana sings against the imminent destruction. A Sumerian song for a dangerous ritual by the earliest female author of world literature

The song is by a high priestess named 'Celestial Ornament' (Enheduana) who lived around 2,300 BC. The brilliantly composed rhetoric was meant for a dangerous ritual which was supposed to stir Inana, the goddess of love and war, to avert the seemingly inevitable doom of a great empire and thus not only the destruction of its ruler and his troops, but also the ignominious death of the author of the song herself. The song evidently became the model for a successful ritual in a desperate situation and can be still understood today as an impressive testament to persevering in hope despite all opposition.

Hallo, W.W./ van Dijk, J.J.A., 'The Exaltation of Inanna', *Yale Near Eastern Researches 3*, New Haven/London 1968 (first edition and interpretation)

Wilcke, C., 'Nin-me-šár-ra – Probleme der Interpretation', *Wiener Zeitschrift für die Kunde des Morgenlandes 68*, 1976, p79–92

Wilcke, C., 'Die Hymne auf das Heiligtum Keš. Zur Struktur und 'Gattung' einer altsumerischen Dichtung und zu ihrer Literaturtheorie', in: Michalowski, P./Veldhuis, N., *Approaches to Sumerian Literature.*

Studies in Honour of Stip (H.L.J. Vanstiphout), Leiden 2005, p201–237 (there p212–213) (interpretation and literary design)

Zgoll, A., 'Der Rechtsfall der En-hedu-Ana im Lied nin-me-šara', *Alter Orient und Altes Testament 246*, Münster 1997 (edition on the basis of new text records, with literal translation and interpretation)

Attinger, P., http://www.arch.unibe.ch/unibe/philhist/iaw/arch/content/e8254/e9161/e241746/4_7_2_ger.pdf (2013) (translation on the basis of new text records, bibliography since 1997)

King Utuhengal expels the Gutians

Utuhengal, king of Uruk, reigning around 2,110 BC, dedicates a monument to his greatest triumph: the victory over the empire of Gutium. Gutium is the name of a people from the Zagros mountains who had already come into Mesopotamia under the mighty dynasty of Akkade and who, after its decline, established a state on the Tigris which claimed supremacy in Mesopotamia for several generations. Utuhengal won back this state for Uruk, one of the old city states of Sumer, with the victory over Tirigan. Utuhengal himself could not found a dynasty – his legacy was taken up by the rulers of the 3rd Dynasty of Ur – but the text of his monument, which he had dedicated to the king of gods Enlil in Nippur, was preserved. This historically important inscription was copied by scholars and thus became part of the traditional texts of Babylonian scholarship. The three copies preserved on clay tablets date to the Old Babylonian Period (19th/18th century BC). The Sumerian text captivates by its literarily artfully composed introduction and the clear prose of the actual report on the campaign.

Frayne, D.R., 'Sargonic and Gutian Periods (2,334–2,113 BC) The Royal Inscriptions of Mesopotamia', *Early Periods 2*, Toronto/ Buffalo/ London 1993, p283–293, no. E2.13.6.4 (most recent text edition with reference to earlier bibliography)

Römer, W.H.PH., 'Zur Siegesinschrift des Königs Utuhengal von Uruk (+/- 2116–2110 v. Chr.)', *Orientalia 54*, 1985, p274–288 (philological edition)

Steinkeller, P., 'New Light on the Hydrology and Topography of Southern Babylonia in the Third Millennium', *Zeitschrift für Assyriologie und Vorderasiatische Archäologie 91*, 2001, p22–84 (on the geography of the places mentioned)

Gilgamesh and Akka

'Gilgamesh and Akka', transmitted from the Old Babylonian Period in Sumerian, reflects in a literary form the conflict between the south of Babylonia (Uruk) and the north (Kish) in the Mesopotamian Early Dynastic Period during the first half of the 3rd millennium BC. Gilgamesh, seeking advice, presents a demand for submission, coupled with the demand for services by Akka, the king of Kish, first to the elders, then to the able-bodied men of his city. While the elders wish to give in to the demand, the young men reject this, which reflects the intentions of the king of Uruk. Gilgamesh emerges victorious from the military confrontation. However, he sets his captured opponent free due to good deeds done to him by Akka previously (granting of asylum?). 'Gilgamesh and Akka' – in contrast to other Sumerian Gilgamesh compositions – did not find its way into the later Akkadian Gilgamesh epic tradition.

Römer, W.H.Ph., 'Das sumerische Kurzepos 'Gilgameš und Akka'. Versuch einer Neubearbeitung', *Alter Orient und Altes Testament 209/1*, Kevelaer/Neukirchen/Vluyn 1980

Electronic Text Corpus of Sumerian Literature 1.8.1.1 [2005]

Katz, D., *Gilgamesh and Akka (LOT 1)*, Groningen 1993 (with further bibliography)

Wilcke, C., 'Zu 'Gilgameš und Akka'. Überlegungen zur Zeit von Entstehung und Niederschrift wie auch zum Text des Epos mit einem Exkurs zur Überlieferung von 'Šulgi A' und von 'Lugalbanda II'', in: Dietrich, M./Loretz, O. (eds), dubsar anta-men. Studien zur Altorientalistik. Festschrift für Willem H.Ph. Römer zur Vollendung seines 70. Lebensjahres mit Beiträgen von Freunden, Schülern und Kollegen, *Alter Orient und Altes Testament 253*, Münster 1998, p457–485

George, A.R., *The Epic of Gilgamesh. The Babylonian Epic Poem and Other Texts in Akkadian and Sumerian*, London 1999, p143–148 (with bibliography)

Birth and Rise of King Sargon

What an ascent: from a boy, born in secret to a high priestess, who was abandoned on the river, to a gardener's apprentice, to ruler of Akkade! The text, written in Akkadian, dates possibly to the reign of King Sargon II of Assyria (722–705 BC), whose equally unexpected rise to ruler of the Assyrian empire should be explained and justified by the comparison with his namesake. The rise of Sargon of Akkade is seen here as inevitable, since the king was both born to a high priestess and chosen by the goddess Ishtar.

Lewis, B., *The Sargon Legend: A Study of the Akkadian Text and The Tale of the Hero who was Exposed at Birth*, American School of Oriental Research, Dissertation Series 4, Cambridge 1980 (edition and compilation of parallels)

Glassner, J.-J., 'Le récit autobiographique de Sargon', *Revue d'Assyriologie 82*, 1988, p1–11 (interpretation)

Westenholz, J.G., *Legends of the Kings of Akkade. The Texts, Mesopotamian Civilizations 7*, Winona Lake 1997, p36–49 (most recent edition of the text)

Dialogue about the indifference of the gods: the Babylonian theodicy

This dialogue is an Akkadian composition in form of an acrostic. In the initial syllables of the 27 strophes of 11 lines each the author has perpetuated himself: 'I am Saggil-kinam-ubbib, the exorcist worshipping god and king'. In the text a 'sufferer' laments his bitter fate despite model moral conduct, as well as the social grievances of his time. His interlocutor, as a representative of the established world view, tries to refute his arguments and to reconcile him with the gods.

Lambert, W.G., *Babylonian Wisdom Literature*, Oxford 1960, p63–91 and p343–345 (publication)

van der Toorn, K., 'Theodicy in Akkadian Literature', in: Laato, A./ de Moor, J.C. (eds), *Theodicy in the World of the Bible*, Leiden/ Boston 2003, p57–89 (comparative study with further bibliography)

From the life of a student

This is a satire in Sumerian that details the laborious daily life of a student from the Old Babylonian Period. School is difficult for the student – although he is making an effort, he is punished again and again. He loses his joy in learning and the situation seems hopeless. Yet a way forward is found: bribing the teacher! Suddenly the alleged good-for-nothing turns into a model student.

The partly free translation is based on the published source texts which were most recently compiled by P. Attinger, http://www.arch.unibe. ch/content/ueber-uns/pascal_attinger/index_ger.html → traductions → Edubbâ 1(5.1.1) 5.1.1. (pdf, 134Kb, 2002, updated 2012)

Edzard, D.O., 'Schulsatiren', in: Charpin, D./Edzard, D.O./Stol, M. (eds), Mesopotamien. Die altbabylonische Zeit, *Annäherungen 4, Orbus Biblicus et Orientalis 160/4*, Göttingen 2004, p531–539.

Glossary

Adad	Semitic weather and storm god
Akka	King of **Kish**, opponent of **Gilgamesh**
Akkade	Capital of the dynasty of the same name (*c.*2320–2170 BC); its location remains unknown
Ammiditana	King of Babylon (*c.*1683–1647 BC)
An(num)	Celestial god and ruler of the gods, father of **Ishtar**, in other traditions her husband in **Uruk**
Anuna/Anunnaku/i	Group of the great gods, later of the underworld
Anzu	Demon with a lion's head and eagle's body, causes sandstorms and other tempests
Apsu	Subterranean fresh water ocean, basis of life, residence of **Ea**
Aruru	Mother and creator goddess
Asushunamir	An Assinnu, member of the Ishtar cult, transsexual, ecstatic, eunuch (?)
Atramhasis	'The exceedingly wise', survivor of the deluge
Belet-ili	'Mistress of the gods', mother deity
Belili	Sister of **Dumuzi**; goddess of fields and crops
Black-headed people	Own description of the Sumerians
Dilmun	Name for Bahrain
Dumuzi	Shepherd god; husband of **Inana**
Eana	'Celestial House', temple of the goddess **Inana** in **Uruk**

112

Ea / Enki	God of fresh water, civilization, wisdom and magic; well-disposed to mankind
Edubba'a	'Clay tablet house', roughly corresponding to a school
Ekur	Main temple of Sumer in **Nippur**; seat of the god **Enlil**
Emmebaragesi	King of **Kish**
Enheduanna	Daughter of King Sargon, high priestess of the moon god **Nanna**/ Suen/ Sin in **Ur**
Enlil	Ruler of the gods, cult place **Nippur**, unpredictable
En priestess	High priestess of any deity
Ennugi	God in charge of dykes and canals
Ereshkigal	Goddess of the underworld
Errakal	Minor god connected with diseases and plagues and **Nergal**
Etana	Sumerian king of **Kish**, ruling after the deluge
Ezinam	Goddess of grain and harvest
Gilgamesh	Legendary king of the city of **Uruk**, hero of the epic with the same name
Gutium	Marauding people in the Zagros mountains
Hubur	River in the underworld
Igigu / Igigi gods	Group of celestial gods
Inan(n)a / Ishtar	Most important goddess of the ancient Near East, goddess of love and war, main cult place **Uruk**
Irkalla	Name of the underworld ruled by **Ereshkigal**
Isin	City in Sumer, city of the goddess of medicine and doctors, **Gula**
Ishkur	Sumerian god of thunderstorms
Kalkal	Minor god, doorkeeper and servant to **Enlil**

Khanish	Minor god, attendant to **Adad**
Kish	Prestigious city in northern Babylonia; according to the Sumerian king list the kingship was established there after the deluge
Kulaba	Part of the city of **Uruk**
Kusarrikum	'Bull man'; protective spirit guarding the entrance of a building
Lahmu	Tutelary god
Lugalane	King of **Uruk** and **Ur**, adversary of the dynasty of **Akkade**
Mami	Mother and creation goddess
Marduk	City god of Babylon, ruler of the gods since the middle of the 2nd millennium BC
mina	Mesopotamian unit of mass with a weight of 497.7g as its ideal value
Namtar(a)	God of the underworld
Nanna	Moon god, city god of **Ur**, **Suen**
Narru	Other name for **Enlil**
Ningal	'Great lady', wife of the moon god **Nanna**/Suen
Ninsumun	Goddess, mother of Gilgamesh
Nintu	Mother goddess
Ninurta	Youthful, martial god
Nippur	Cult capital of Sumer, cult place of **Enlil**
Nisaba	Goddess of writing and grain
Nusku	Vizier of **Enlil**
Papsukkal	Minister of the gods
Qadištum	Priestess
Sargon	Founder of the Dynasty of **Akkade** (from *c.*2320 BC), having become legendary through unusual deeds

Sebettu	Group of seven good and seven evil demons
Sin/ Suen	Moon god and city god of **Ur**
Shamash/ Utu	Solar god and god of judgement
Sheshgal	'Big brother' in the clay tablet house, mentor and supervisor for the younger students
Sharrabu	Fever demon
Shullat	Minor god, attendant to **Adad**
Sumer	The south of modern Iraq
Ur	City in the south of Iraq, cult place of the moon god **Nanna**/Suen
Urash	Earth goddess
Uruk	Most important city in the south of Iraq, cult place of **Inana**/Ishtar and of **An**(um)
Ushumgalana	Another name for **Dumuzi**
Utuhengal	King of city of **Uruk**, *c.*2110 BC
We	Rebellious god
Zulummaru	Another name of **Ea**/Enki

Chronological Table

(for rough orientation)

Around 3200 BC	Invention of writing in Uruk
c.2700–2300	Time of the city states
c.2320–2170	Supremacy of the Dynasty of Akkade; important kings are Sargon and Naram-Suen
c.2200–2110	Raids of the Gutians, instability
c.2110–2000	3rd Dynasty of Ur, beginning of the scripting of Sumerian literature
c.2000–1595	Old Babylonian Period: unification of Babylonia, normative period
c.1580–1155	Time of the Cassites in Babylonia
From c.1400	Rise of the Assyrian empire
884–612	Neo-Assyrian Period (Assyrian empire): Assurnasirpal II (883–859), Sargon II (721–705), Assurbanipal (668– c.630, library)
605–539	Neo-Babylonian Period (Ishtar gate in Babylon, Nebuchadnezzar II, Nabonid)
539	Conquest of Babylon by Cyrus II of Persia, loss of independence
75 AD	Last known cuneiform text

The authors

Hannelore Agnethler initially studied Protestant Theology, then Ancient Near Eastern Studies at the Ludwig-Maximilians-University in Munich. One focus of her interest is the crossover of religious conceptions between the world of the ancient Near East and that of the Old Testament.

Marc Elsässer is studying Ancient Near Eastern Studies at the Ludwig-Maximilians-University in Munich. He places particular emphasis on (Semitic) linguistics and is about to finish his BA.

Sabina Franke teaches ancient Near Eastern Studies at the University of Hamburg, the Helmut-Schmidt-University in Hamburg and the Paris-Lodron-University in Salzburg. In particular she offers general sessions for students of all subjects. Her research interests lie in the general cultural history of the Ancient Near East.

Hans Neumann studied Near Eastern Archaeology and Philology at the Martin-Luther-University in Halle-Wittenberg. After his doctorate at the Academy of Sciences of the German Democratic Republic in Berlin and post-doctoral work at the Free University Berlin (1998), he has been professor for Ancient Near Eastern Philology and director of the Institute for Ancient Near Eastern Philology and Near Eastern Archaeology at the Westphalian Wilhelms-University in Münster since 1999. His interests include the economic, legal and social history of the ancient Near East as well as Sumerian literature.

Rosel Pientka-Hinz taught from 2004 to 2010 as lecturer for Ancient Near Eastern Studies at the University of Marburg; in 2007–08 she was visiting professor at the University of Vienna. Since then, besides her work as a private lecturer at the University of Marburg, she has taught in Bochum and Berlin. In 2009–10 she researched the importance of snakes in the ancient Near East as a fellow at the Käte-Hamburger-College 'Dynamics of the religious history between Asia and Europe' at the University of Bochum. Focal points of her research are text transmissions in the Old Babylonian Period; the cultural and religious history of the ancient Near East (cult and magic, mythology, flora and fauna, architecture, colour categories and forms of perception).

Walther Sallaberger is holder of the chair for Assyriology at the Ludwig-Maximilians-University in Munich. Among his current topics of research are studies on Sumerian, especially its lexicon, and on the history of Mesopotamia in the third millennium.

Karin Stella Schmidt studied Ancient Near Eastern Philology, Near Eastern Archaeology and Classical Archaeology; subsequently she worked as contract teacher, research associate and academic counsellor at the universities of Freiburg, Heidelberg and Würzburg. Bilingualism in Mesopotamia, Sumerian-Akkadian literature, the history of religion and music and 'Hellenism in the East' are among her areas of research.

Michael P. Streck is professor for Ancient Near Eastern Studies at the University of Leipzig. Together with Nathan Wasserman of the Hebrew University in Jerusalem he is working on a corpus of the early Babylonian-Assyrian literature (www.seal.uni-leipzig.de).

Annette Zgoll is professor for Ancient Near Eastern Studies at the Georg-August-University in Göttingen. Priorities in her research are Sumerian and Babylonian-Assyrian myths, as well as the literature and religion of ancient Mesopotamia.